The Mystery of Deadly Daisies
Steven Vagovics

I.

Honolulu, Hawaii
4 March 1947

The night was falling down to a late midnight hour. Two friends, Frank and Daniel, were just leaving the local bar called Lopez Hills. With a high level of alcohol in their veins, they were walking around and talking.

- Are you going straight home, Frank, or are you going to visit Marge first?
- I will probably go and see Marge first. I do not think she will be happy to see me like this, though.
- Tell her that I still do not know anything about the jewels.
- Gee, I told you a thousand times already, they belong to her and not to you!
- They belong to me! She just took them from me!
- Give her a break! She's your sister, man! The testament gave her the same rights to your mother's possessions as it did to you!
- That doesn't mean she can just take them from me! I worked hard for that jewelry. I'll even sue her, if necessary!

Frank got a burst of anger when he heard these words.

- You didn't do anything for them! Please, just leave me alone. I don't want to argue with you now!
- You just say that because she's your girlfriend! You would agree with me if it wasn't so!
- That's not true!
- You bet it is! In addition, you can't even admit that you're interested about their value, too!

Suddenly, Frank didn't know what Daniel was talking about. That was because only Daniel knew about the true value of the jewels of his mother.

- You're just a hypocrite, you know that, Frank?
- That's enough! Get out of my sight!

Daniel left and Frank was heading to his car. As he was pulling out his car keys, a mysterious man appeared in the darkness, dressed in a brown suit. From the distance, he was speaking to Frank.

- Do you really want to continue playing games?

Frank looked around.

- Yes, I'm talking to you, Frank Lombardo.

Frank got scared stiff and with a fear in his voice, he answered the question.

-    Please, sir! I don't know about anything! How do you know my name?

The man continued.

-    I know a lot about you! That's why you have to pay!

Frank, being drunk, only saw a silhouette of a man walking fast towards him. When he saw a knife in his hands, he began to shout from his entire lungs.

-    No, please don't do it, I beg you!

The man stabbed Frank three times in his stomach. As his body was lying on the ground, entirely soaked in blood, the man put a piece of daisy next to his head. Afterwards, he quickly ran away. Frank's dead body stayed lying there.

II.

The Police Station
4 March 1947

It was a busy day at the Police Department of Honolulu.

Lieutenant Phil More had just heard about the murder nearby the Lopez Hills Bar. He immediately called two detectives into his office.

One of them was Herbie Fox. Lieutenant More knew that he was perfect for this case. Herbie was a sixty-year-old man who had forty years of investigative experience. He loved his job, although he didn't make it show on the outside. Herbie was a stronger man with his hair going grey and with a scar on his cheek. He was usually rude to people, which might had been because of his age and cynicism, which may seemed typical for people like him.

The second detective was Albert Fringe, who was a middle-aged man who had just been promoted to a higher department. Even though he had a lot of medical problems, he believed in himself and tried to be the best detective he could possibly be. His body was fit, his hair was ginger and he had freckles on his face, which possessed somewhat of a pale characteristics.

The lieutenant spoke with them.

- Greetings, fellas. I have some bad news for you.

The lieutenant had not even finished his sentence and Herbie asked a question with sarcasm in his voice already.

- Is it about some murder again?

The lieutenant smiled and answered.

- You just can't let me have the joy of telling you, can you?

Herbie smiled with a charming look on his face. Nevertheless, Albert joined the conversation with a serious manner.

- What's the matter, lieutenant?
- We got a report that there was a murder near the Lopez Hills Bar. Officer Shelby found a dead body on a parking lot nearby. You should go there and investigate the crime scene.

Suddenly, Herbie got angry.

- Do you want to send both of us there? I don't even know this man. I prefer to work alone, as you might surely know.

Albert got upset and the lieutenant stated with anger.

- For crying out loud, don't be so cold, Fox! The man standing by your side is one of the best young detectives we have here! I'm sure you'll get along just fine.

Herbie answered with a calmer tone of his voice.

- With all due respect, lieutenant: if you saw such a load of dead bodies as I have in your life, you would be glad to have my kind of personality.

Afterwards, Herbie looked at Albert and apologized for making a scene.

- I'm sorry, mister... What's your name?
- Albert Fringe. Pleased to meet you, mister Fox. I'm your admirer and I really respect what you do. You're my idol.

Herbie laughed and replied.

- I advise you to go and work in that new restaurant, which got opened a few days ago. You can buy a beef for as low as one cent there!

Albert started laughing from the bottom of his heart and the situation in the office started to look witty. Even the lieutenant started to laugh. After a little while, the conversation continued.

- It didn't even take a minute and you two are good friends already! Are you happy now, mister Fox?
- Oh yes, lieutenant. Obviously, this fella has a good sense of humor.
- All right then, Fox, you should now go and start investigating. Time is precious, you know.

Herbie and Albert left the building and got into a car. Albert was the driver. During the commute, they had a conversation. Herbie started.

- I need to tell you something about myself, mister Fringe. Something about my personality.
- I'm listening, mister Fox.
- I have a few personal conditions during the investigations, which you should respect.
- Which ones, for instance?
- To start off, I'm an introvert. I keep a lot of my thought processes purely to myself. You should know that, mister Fringe.
- Of course, mister Fox. After all, I'm not that different from you.

Herbie looked at Albert with a surprise in his eyes.

- Believe me, mister Fringe. We are two completely different people. I'll bet my life that this is so!

After a moment of silence, Herbie continued.

- What motivated you to detective work, mister Fringe? Were you expecting to bring some excitement into your life?
- I wouldn't say so, mister Fox. I was always interested in being a detective so, I decided to go for it after I graduated from the high school in Connecticut; I wanted to fulfill my dreams.
- Your dreams? About what? Looking at the dead bodies and interrogating psychopaths?
- I don't know what lead me here. It was just a feeling I had, which I couldn't hide.
- Just look at that! Only a few minutes of knowing you and I know about one of your life dreams already. At least you got it fulfilled. I only hope that you won't have to face disappointment in your life.
- Did you face it?
- I can't really tell, mister Fringe. Have you ever seen a dead body?
- No.
- Well, prepare for a moment of truth then. You'll finally see what it is to be a detective. As soon as that moment appears, you'll understand what I'm talking about.

Albert remained calm.

III.

The Crime Scene
4 March 1947

After a few minutes, Albert and Herbie arrived at the Lopez Hills Bar. Journalists and police officers had surrounded the area. Albert and Herbie came close to the police line.

- Detectives?

Asked one of the police officers who stood near the line. Herbie showed him his badge. The police officer looked at it and said.

- Oh, I see. We've been expecting you, mister Fox! You can cross the line.

Herbie said jokingly.

- I wonder why you haven't recognized me, officer Blake.

Officer Blake got a little upset. Then, Herbie and Albert crossed the line. When they made a few steps, there was the dead body of Frank Lombardo lying next to them, with an analytic, Dean Marston, who was bent down and observing it. He was an old man with dyed brown hair, round glasses, wearing a white braid. He had rough wrinkles on his face and a fit figure. Even though he had a tough job, he was always calm by nature. He suffered from a mild level of lisp. Albert got scared stiff and nervous when he saw the body. Herbie grabbed his shoulder and whispered into his ears.

- This is how it feels like to be a detective. Welcome to my world! Keep in mind; the worst things in your life are still yet to come, my friend.

Afterwards, Herbie started talking with Dean.

- What have you got so far, mister Marston?
- Hello, mister Fox. The victim has quite a lot of wounds. Three of them are in the area of his stomach. It's apparent that a knife stabbed him. He simply fell down to the ground and bled out. The daisy placed next to the body is artificial.
- Does he have wounds anywhere else on his body?
- There are some red spots on his neck. What that means is: it's possible that the victim has been strangled before being stabbed to death. I'll need to analyze the whole body in my laboratory for more detailed assumptions. It also looks like the victim has been under the influence of alcohol.
- Thank you, mister Marston.

Dean stood up and observed the crime scene a little further. Herbie bent down to the body and started looking for some clues. He looked into the pockets of a coat, which Frank wore that night. He could feel some papers in them, so he pulled them out of there. The first one was a card of a man called Malfred Ash with his telephone number and an address written on it. Herbie immediately took a note of both, the telephone number and the address, into his notebook. The next paper in Frank's coat pockets was a letter from a caretaker, which informed Frank about a late mortgage payment. Herbie took a note of the caretaker's name: Charlie Crown. Besides the papers, there were three bonbons, apartment keys, and a wallet in his pockets. The wallet had a total of thirty dollars in it. Herbie stood up and observed the crime scene with Albert walking by his side. Albert asked.

- Have you found out anything?
- Not really. There are not a lot of clues here. The most interesting thing may be the car key inserted in his car.
- Why do you think so? It only has Frank's fingerprints and maybe fingerprints of some of his relatives. I don't see anything special about them.
- Don't be so narrow-minded, mister Fringe! They might help us in some situations, maybe tell us something more.
- I'm not so sure about that but, so be it, mister Fox.

Herbie put a white glove on his hand and took the car keys. Afterwards, he carefully placed them in a small plastic bag. Later, Herbie decided to visit the Lopez Hills Bar. There was an obese man with short black hair behind the bar counter.

Herbie and Albert came close to him and Herbie started talking.

- Detective Herbie Fox, I would like to ask you a few questions.

The barkeeper replied with more of a rude manner.

- All right, go on. What do you want?

Herbie sat on a barstool. Albert was just standing and watching. Herbie started talking.

- We are investigating a murder, which happened near your bar. Could you describe to me precisely what happened last night? Does the name Frank Lombard ring any bell to you?
- Lombardo? Yes, I know that guy. He's one of my regulars. What about him?
- I'm unfortunate to say this... He was murdered yesterday. Did he have problems with alcohol?
- Gee! What a cruel world! It depends. Sometimes he came and drank one glass of vodka; sometimes he came and nearly poisoned himself with almost everything liquid we had here. I don't think he actually had drinking problems, though. He wasn't drinking alcohol each and every time he came here, you know.

- That sounds interesting. Was he alone or did he have a company?
- He was here with a friend. I think his name was Daniel Greg. They were arguing a lot, though. At one point, they nearly got into a fistfight and at the other one; they were drinking Martini with laughter together.

Herbie took a note of this information. He started thinking.

- Do you know what might have been the cause of their argument?
- I was hearing things about some woman called Marge, but I also heard something about diamonds.
- What diamonds?
- I don't know. My memory is kind of shaky about that.
- Try to remember! It can help the investigation by a mile in some situation.
- I can recall some argument about who shall possess them. I can't remember anything more right now. Maybe it was only a drunk talk.

Herbie continued taking notes. Albert started asking questions, too.

- Can you tell us when did they leave?
- It could be about three o'clock in the morning.
- Did you hear any noise?
- No, I didn't hear anything.

Albert got suspicious.

- How come? It happened not even a mile away from your bar!

The barkeeper got nervous and started looking to sides. He stated with anger.

- All right, I did. I heard shouting and then a strange weeping noise.
- Why did you not do anything?
- I'm just an ordinary barkeeper! I hear shouting men every night, for crying out loud!

Herbie started to ask questions again.

- Why didn't you call the police?
- I didn't find it necessary.

Herbie stood up from his chair and let his temper show out.

- Go and take a look outside! There's a dead man who didn't deserve to die! You might have helped him to his grave with your ignorance!
- Stop shouting at me! Otherwise, I'll make a complaint about you two assholes!
- You must have such a fugitive mind, mister barkeeper.

The barkeeper raised his voice furiously.

- That's enough! Get the hell out of my bar and leave me alone!

Herbie replied with sarcasm.

- It was a pleasure being here, mister barkeeper. I hope I'll be able to come here again sometime.

The barkeeper shouted.

- Screw you, chump!

Even though it looked like Herbie and Albert were about to leave the bar, the argument between Herbie and the barkeeper continued for several minutes. It came to the point when Albert simply couldn't take it anymore and he pulled a pack of cigarettes out of his pocket. Afterwards, he announced.

- I'm going to have a cigarette outside, if you don't mind.

Albert went outside and lit up his cigarette. When he finished smoking, he wanted to throw the stub into a trash bin as he didn't want to simply throw it on the ground. He found one at the backside of the bar. When he reached the trash bin, he noticed something sharp beneath the garbage. He gently grabbed and picked out an object. It was wrapped in a black bag. While he was softly unwrapping the object in his hands, he got terrified. He could see drops of blood. When he unwrapped the object completely, it was obvious. It was a bloody knife! He wrapped the knife back into the black bag with terror and ran to Herbie. The argument was still going on when he entered the bar. Albert shouted.

- Mister Fox, I found something very questionable outside! I want to show it to you in private, though.

Herbie replied with a light smile.

- What is it? A golden coin or what?

Albert remained nervous and replied seriously.

- No, it's something serious! I really need you to see it.
- All right then. I'll just say goodbye to my friend here.

Herbie smiled at the barkeeper who had a very angry look on his face.

- Goodbye, my friend. I hope we can have a chat sometime soon again.

Herbie stated to the barkeeper. As they both came to the entrance, he added.

- Mister barkeeper, before I leave, I would like to give you a riddle.

The barkeeper hesitated but agreed. Herbie continued.

- A drink spilling out makes one person annoying and desperate at the same time. Who is that person?

The barkeeper thought about it for a while but remained silent. After a while, Herbie stated.

- It's a beloved barkeeper, my friend!

The barkeeper got surprised and Albert laughed. Herbie and Albert left the bar. As they were going to the car, Albert said.

- I wouldn't say that you have such a good sense of humor, mister Fox!

Herbie replied with confidence.

- Extraordinary problems require extraordinary solutions, mister Fringe! What do you want to show me?

Albert showed the knife to Herbie.

- I found this at the backside of the bar. Take a look at it.

Herbie got surprised and stated with joy.

- Well, well, well! This must be the knife that killed the victim. This is outstanding! You have found a major clue! I'm starting to be glad that they assigned you to me. I wouldn't find this one myself!

Albert smiled.

- It was nothing, mister Fox. I've noticed it by a pure coincidence when I wanted to throw a cigarette stub to the trash bin.
- We need to deliver this object to the analysis!

IV.

The Police Station
4 March 1947

Herbie and Albert arrived at the police station. Herbie had the wrapped knife in his hands and he spoke to the doorkeeper.

- Good afternoon, Mike. I'm looking for mister Marston. Is he in his laboratory?
- He has just finished the analysis of the dead body a few minutes ago. He should be in the canteen right now. You'll probably have to wait a while.
- Thank you, Mike.

Herbie and Albert sat down and waited. Herbie started a new conversation.

- What do you think about the detective work so far, mister Fringe?
- Actually, I don't have a certain opinion yet. What I can say is that some things almost made me throw up.
- That's understandable, mister Fringe.
- Can I ask you about your beginnings?

Herbie smiled and replied.

- I can recall them quite precisely. I was twenty years old and I was just finishing the police academy. My mother was a police officer. I had a job almost immediately after my graduation.

Albert nodded his head and Herbie continued.

- I remember my first serious case. It was a murder of a clockmaker. When I solved it, the lieutenant took a fancy of me. When there was an opportunity, he always gave me awards for being the best detective. Thinking about it, it all might have happened because of my poor mother.

Herbie started to look around, stuck in his thoughts. After a little while, Dean Marston appeared. Herbie stopped him and spoke with him.

- Mister Marston, are you available right now? We have an important clue that needs to be analyzed.
- Of course. What clue?
- Let's go.

They all walked into the Dean Marston's laboratory and closed the door. Herbie started to gently unwrap the knife from the black bag. A few seconds later, the knife got revealed and Marston took an astonishing glance at it. Herbie stated.

- This one.

Marston observed it for a little moment and stated.

- Interesting. Where did you find it?
- Mister Fringe found it in a trash bin.

24

- Have you touched the unwrapped parts with your hands?

Albert replied.

- No, I haven't. I've strictly touched the black bag only.

Dean claimed with a slight relief.

- That's great! I can identify the fingerprints without inspecting yours first. Supposing the killer wasn't wearing gloves, of course. I can conduct that he had more courage than intelligence. Murdering someone with a knife and throwing it into the nearest trash bin isn't something that you can get away with, you see.

Herbie started thinking out loud.

- I guess that this case might be already solved. The murderer's fingerprints are on the knife. We'll arrest him and there we go!

Dean stated.

- Not so fast, mister Fox! I don't think he wasn't wearing gloves. Also, there might be fingerprints of more people on that knife.

Herbie argued.

- I'm not concluding anything. I don't rely on fingerprints, anyway. I'm creating my own opinions mainly by the interrogations. Fingerprints always help, though. It depends on how successful your analysis will be. Anyway, I've heard that you have finished the analysis of the dead body. What have you got?

Marston came to the white awning. He grabbed his analysis documents. After a little while, he started explaining.

-   I have some rather interesting results. My guess that the victim was under the influence of alcohol was confirmed. There were also particles of nicotine in his body. There are bruises on his chest and several other ones throughout his entire body. Some of those look like they were caused by glass. Probably a bar incident, I might say.

Herbie asked curiously.

-   Could you describe those bruises in more detail?
-   Quite apparent and deep. You see it looks like someone beat him up, which only adds to my theory of a bar incident. There are also some signs of a black eye. Talking about it, could you please give me that knife? This won't be pretty, though.

As Herbie was giving the knife to Dean, he asked Albert.

-   Will you be able to handle this, mister Fringe?

Albert replied calmly.

-   I hope so. I have already seen the body.

Herbie nodded his head softly and stated.

-   All right, you have been warned then. You can continue, mister Marston.

Dean revealed the body slowly. Albert got terrified and almost threw up again. Herbie remained calm and the sight in front of him didn't cause anything to him. Dean placed the knife on the victim's stomach and concluded.

-   It's obvious. The wound is matching the shape of this knife! I'm almost certain that the blood is the victims. We have our answer. Right here is the murder weapon! I don't think we need analysis anymore, as you might see now.

Herbie replied.

-   Thank you, mister Marston. If you find out anything new, call and leave a message for Lieutenant More. He'll forward it to me during the next call to the police station.
-   Of course, mister Fox. My services are here for you.
-   Have a nice day, mister Marston.
-   Have a nice day, too, mister Fox.

Herbie and Albert left the laboratory room. During their walking through the police station, Lieutenant More stopped them.

-   Mister Fox, we have a witness here!

Herbie replied with a surprise.

- Which room?
- Interrogation Room two.
- Thank you, Lieutenant More. Let's go, mister Fringe!

They entered the room and Albert closed the door. There was an old lady sitting at the table. She had a very calm and quiet voice. Herbie sat down in front of her and started the interrogation. Albert stood by his side and after he had been given an order, he transcribed the whole conversation.

- Detective Fox, so what can you tell us about this case, missis...?
- Angie, Angie Rothford. I am the neighbor of Frank Lombardo.

Herbie seemed to be joyous about this fact.

- I'm very glad that you came here. You can begin your testimony now.

Missis Rothford started explaining.

- The incident happened at around three o'clock in the morning. I woke up to the strange noises outside and I looked outside the window. I saw my neighbor, Frank Lombardo.
- Can you describe the person's appearance that was with him?

- My memory is not in such a good shape, mister. I wonder how I even recognized the face of Lombardo. I remember that they were walking past the street and they were arguing about some diamonds. Unfortunately, that's all my memory can come up with.
- All right, missis Rothford. Can you tell me something more about Frank Lombardo?
- I didn't know him well. He sometimes came to visit me and he even helped me with groceries, time after time. Anyway, I noticed that he had problems with the caretaker. He didn't have a lot of money and he often had difficulties with paying the mortgage, you know.
- We've acknowledged some of these things already. Can you tell us something more, missis Rothford?
- I wish I could, but I'm afraid I can't. I'll probably disappoint you with that. I just wanted to tell you what I know. I thought it might help you a little.

Herbie stood up.

- Thank you, missis Rothford. You're a prime example of how each citizen of Honolulu should act.
- Kind words, Detective. Goodbye.
- Goodbye.

Herbie and Albert left the room and headed outside the building towards the car. Soon afterwards, missis Rothford left, too. When Herbie and Albert entered the car, Albert asked.

- What now, mister Fox?
- I think we're about to visit our victim's company. Oh, I need to get his address. Wait here, mister Fringe.

Herbie got out of the car and accessed the nearest telephone booth.

- Operator, Detective Herbie Fox speaking. I need you to connect me with the Social Security Administration of Honolulu.
- Wait, please.

After a few seconds of bleeping, a voice of a woman spoke to the telephone.

- Social Security Administration of Honolulu. How can I help you?
- Detective Herbie Fox at the telephone. I need an address of a man called Daniel Greg.
- Moment.

After a little while, the voice of the woman spoke again.

- There are more people under the name Daniel Greg in our database. Do you have some specific information about this person?
- Which one of them lives closest to the Harding Avenue?

- There is one person who lives almost on that street. 3266A Lincoln Avenue; Honolulu, HI 96816

Herbie took a note of the address to his notebook.

- Thank you.

He hung up the telephone and returned to the car. Albert asked him.

- Do you have it, mister Fox?
- Yes, I do. Let's hope that it's Daniel Greg we're looking for.
- Are you not sure?
- There were more people under that name in the database. I've asked for the address of the one who lives closest to the Lopez Hills Bar.
- That was a wise decision, I suppose, mister Fox.
- You probably know what to do.

V.

Daniel Greg
4 March 1947

Herbie showed Albert a note of the address. Albert hit the pedal and drove there. After a few minutes later, they arrived. There was a smaller house and they both reached the door. When Herbie rang the doorbell, a man with longer brown hair and a fit figure opened up.

- Who are you?

Herbie took his badge and said.

- Detective Herbie Fox. This is my detective partner. His name is Albert Fringe. We have some questions about last night.

Daniel got surprised.

- Come in.

Both of them entered the house and sat down on a sofa in the living room. Daniel was getting more and more terrified every second.

- What happened, detectives?

Herbie and Albert looked at each other. After a little while, Herbie started talking.

-   We're investigating a murder of Frank Lombardo.

Daniel got shocked and asked with horror.

-   I hope you don't want to tell me... I mean, I just really don't know what... Are you telling me that he's dead?
-   I'm afraid so, mister Greg.

Daniel covered his face with his palms and started breathing heavily. After a while, he continued.

-   That can't be so! Please say it's not true! Dammit, Frank! What happened?
-   We found him dead by his car. Someone stabbed him to death and he bled out.
-   No! Why him? This is just... unbelievable!

Daniel stood up and walked through the room nervously. Herbie continued.

-   I know it's hard for you, but we need to ask you some questions.

Daniel slightly calmed down and sat down on the sofa again. Calm but still shocked, he said.

-   I'm listening.
-   Albert, you know what to do.

Herbie gave his notebook to Albert who was already pulling out his pen out of his pocket. Herbie started the conversation.

34

- Tell me in detail, what happened yesterday in the bar. We have information that you were with the victim until approximately three o'clock in the morning.
- There's not that much to tell about yesterday. We were both tired from work. We arranged to go to the bar and relax a little.
- Describe to me the whole evening.
- Nothing interesting. We came there at about eight o'clock and ordered out first piña colada. Since then, the time just flew by and we didn't even know what time it was.
- Was Frank involved in a bar fight?
- No, he wasn't. Why are you asking that?
- He had several different bruises on his body.
- Really? I don't know how he got them.
- How was your relationship with Frank?
- We were good friends for years. We played golf together, went to a lot of events, and we met each other in the bar every Friday night.
- Did you have any conflicts with him?
- Things got a little out of control when he started dating my sister, Marge. Otherwise, we had no conflicts.

Herbie looked skeptically at Albert and asked more questions.

- We got some testimonies about diamonds. Did you have some property issues between each other?

Suddenly, Daniel started to slightly shake.

- I don't know what you're talking about.

Herbie began raising his voice.

- Well, that's quite interesting, mister Greg. In our testimonies, a witness stated that you were arguing about jewelry. Does it not ring a bell to you?

Daniel started to shake a little more intensively.

- No, I don't know anything.

Herbie chose to be ruder.

- Mister Greg, I'd like to warn you that giving false statements to the police is a federal crime in this country! You can even spend years in prison!

Daniel couldn't handle the pressure anymore and he started admitting.

- Ok, ok, you got me. Things are more complicated around that.
- Go on.
- The thing was, my mother died just a few weeks ago. You can't stop the time; you know how it goes. Her testament is not entirely clear and she owned quite some valuable pieces of jewelry. Since I'm her firstborn child, I think it should be me who gets to own them. Marge doesn't think that, though. She thinks that something like diamond jewelry should

get to the daughter. To be honest, we had so many arguments that we haven't even talked since the day of my mother's funeral.

Herbie got suspicious and claimed.

- Something's fishy about this, mister Greg. Do you want to tell me that you have some serious feuds with your own sister just because of some decorative objects? I think that those jewelry pieces have some higher value, which only you know about. You want to own the diamonds to make a good barter.
- That's not true! Stop accusing me!

Although Daniel wanted to defend himself, he knew that Herbie concluded his intentions perfectly. He wanted to stand up and make the detectives leave but he couldn't do that due to his softer character. Herbie carried on with his speech.

- You know what, mister Greg? I think I have just revealed the first suspect of Frank's murder! Without even saying that much, you have made me imagine the murder's motive.
- Please stop! What you're saying doesn't make any sense! We were good friends! I had no reason to kill him! Furthermore, it was my sister who I have a feud with, not him. How did you even think of that?

Herbie hit the table with his fist and started shouting. Albert got slightly scared because of his scene.

- Where did you go last night when you left Frank? You must have heard his crying! Did you disappear like some Canterville ghost?
- I quickly went away. I was strongly drunk, so you can be glad that I even remember something.
- Let's go, mister Fringe, but one more thing. Give me an address of your sister. If you give us a false one, we'll come back and bring you downtown!

Daniel started looking nervously after a piece of paper and a pen. Albert offered him the notebook with his pen.

- You can write it down here. Try to write it as clearly as possible, please.
- Thank you.

When he finished writing, he gave the notebook back to Albert. Herbie came to the door with threatful words.

- I have my eyes on you, mister Greg!

Herbie opened the door and left. Albert followed him. Daniel got very upset and didn't say a word.

VI.

Marge Greg
4 March 1947

Herbie and Albert got in the car. Albert cranked up the engine and while driving, he asked Herbie.

-   Was it necessary, mister Fox?

Herbie replied with confidence.

-   Being a detective is not an easy task, mister Fringe. Sometimes you just have to get out of your comfort zone and act fiercely.
-   But you know, he didn't show any signs of resisting, and he was cooperating with us.
-   I don't know if you heard the same things as I did, mister Fringe. He tried to lie to us! If we didn't have any previous testimonies, we still wouldn't have a single suspect.
-   And what about that barkeeper? Did you find him at least a bit suspicious?
-   Nothing is impossible. I keep an eye out on everyone who has something to do with the victim. That applies to each case. Nevertheless, the only suspect at the moment is Daniel Greg.
-   Can I ask you why? It is true that he only had a feud with his sister and not him.

- It may seem illogical. You see, one thing remains the same on the testimony. As you remember, he told us that Frank was dating Daniel's sister before his death. Try to think about it the way I do. There are tons of possibilities and hypotheses about this. What if Lombardo had something to do with the diamonds, too? What if he had a plan with Marge based on those diamonds? Do you understand what I'm trying to say, mister Fringe?
- I have a clearer picture in my mind already.
- I doubt that Daniel told us the whole truth. Something just seems to be wrong with him. I don't like that.

After a few minutes, they arrived at a place where Marge Greg was supposed to live. It was a six-story apartment. Herbie looked at the mailboxes. When he saw Marge Greg written on one of them, he stated with a mild laughter.

- Daniel didn't give us a fake address, at least.

They entered the building and started looking for the story on which was Marge. Herbie suggested.

- I'll take a look on the left door, you'll take a look on the right door. Is it okay for you?
- Yes, it is, mister Fox.

They walked across the first story, then the second, third, fourth. On the fifth, Albert found a tag of Marge Greg.

- Here she is!
- Great, mister Fringe.

Herbie knocked on the door. After a while, an attractive, approximately 40-year-old woman opened the door. She had long blonde hair and blue eyes. She was very fit and she had a soft voice. She looked at the detectives with horror in her eyes and asked.

- Who are you?
- Detective Herbie Fox. This is my detective partner, Albert Fringe. We would like to ask you a few questions.

With a surprise and not saying a word, she let them both into her flat. When they sat down on her sofa, she asked a question.

- Would you like something to drink?
- No, thank you. Sit down, please.
- As you say so, mister Fox.

She sat down on the sofa and Herbie started talking.

- We're investigating a murder of Frank Lombardo. Could you please tell us where were you last night? Do you know something about yesterday's arrangements of Frank Lombardo and Daniel Greg?

With tears in her eyes, she wondered.

- Frank... Frank is dead?
- I'm afraid so, missis Greg.

Marge started crying with her face covered in her palms. After a while, Herbie and Albert started looking at each other. Herbie decided to calm down Marge.

- Listen to me, Marge. I do realize that this is a big tragedy for you, but we need as much information from you to solve the case of his murder and catch the murderer. So please, answer me, Marge. What can you tell us about Frank and Daniel's night out yesterday?

Marge started wiping out tears from her face with her hands but she could only speak with crying.

- I know... I know that... I know that they went to the bar. Frank called me and told me that he was going there with Daniel and that he was coming to visit me afterwards. He also told me that he might go home, so I didn't get nervous when he wasn't arriving.
- Can you describe Frank?
- Do you mean his character and things like that?
- Yes, missis Marge. I'm deeply sorry for your loss.
- Frank... I don't know how to describe him. People had mixed opinions about him. If I were to generalize, I would possibly say that he was a weirdo.
- What exactly do you mean by that?

- He had a quite strange attitude towards things. He was even mysterious in some ways. For instance, he never told me a lot about his intentions in certain situations. It may sound strange, but this was one of the reasons why I loved him so much. Sometimes he even scared me with his behavior. At other times, he had mood swings and was a bit aggressive. It was never anything serious, though.
- Can you tell me more about your relationship?
- We dated for over a year. He even proposed to me, but I rejected it. I wanted to marry him after solving all his financial issues.
- Financial issues?
- Yes, you see, he was an electrician. He could just barely pay the rent and sometimes, he even had to borrow money from his mother in order to do it.
- Could you give me an address of his mother?
- You'll need to wait for a moment. I'll fetch my phone book.

Marge stood up from her chair. After a while, she brought her phone book and put it on the table. She started looking for a piece of paper. Herbie told Albert.

- You know what to do.

Albert gave the notebook to Marge with the same words as the last time.

- Try to write it as clearly as possible, please.

Marge wrote down the address and returned the pen and notebook to Albert.

- Here you are.

Herbie continued.

- Thank you, missis Marge. We shall continue now. There is one question that bothers me the most. What can you tell us about the diamonds?
- What diamonds?

Herbie looked at Marge with anger.

- Don't play any games with us, missis Marge. I'm talking about the diamonds, which caused your brother and you to have a feud.
- Oh, yes, I know. Excuse me. I didn't know what diamonds you're talking about at first.

Herbie gave a scorned expression and stated.

- Tell me everything you know about the diamonds. I know it's complicated, but we need to hear your version.
- Our mother, Evelyn, died a few weeks ago. She owned a lot of diamonds. I was born after my brother and he found out that her will does not say anything about who shall get the diamonds.
- Do you know something about the value those diamonds might have?

- I'm not very good at these things. I don't think they are valuable very much, but maybe I'm wrong. On the other hand, my brother is greedy for money. I'm afraid that he might sell them right away when he gets them. It wouldn't be fair to our mother. She treasured them like gold for her entire life! Needless to say, I think that my brother will forcefully get them and I won't be able to do anything about it.
- So you don't know anything about their value?
- Not a financial one. Still, they mean a lot to me since my mother treasured them so much throughout her life.

Herbie looked at the ground and mumbled.

- That son of a bitch!

Marge got surprised and asked.

- Pardon?
- I'm sorry, missis Marge. I have a feeling that your brother is keeping something in secret.
- Like what?
- To be honest, I think that your brother wants those diamonds because of their value. Is there some connection between Frank and the diamonds?
- Well, sort of. In my mother's will, there is a statement, which says that the child who is married should inherit more.
- And you claim that you did want to marry Frank.

- Yes, I did. I only refused his proposal because of the complicated situations going on right now.
- I see. Is your brother married, missis Marge?
- He got divorced two years ago. Hannah is now his ex-wife.
- It's not easy for me to say this, missis Marge, but the future of your brother looks questionable.
- Please tell me you're not seeing him as a suspect of Frank's murder!
- I'm sorry, missis Marge, but yes. After hearing the testimonies, there is a cloud of doubt over the innocence of your brother.

Herbie stood up and looked around the room. Meanwhile, he told Albert.

- It looks like we're moving on, mister Fringe.

Herbie came to the door and said.

- Thank you, missis Marge. Take care of yourself.

As he was closing the door, Marge came and added with fear.

- Wait, mister Fox.
- Yes, missis Marge?
- Promise me you won't arrest my brother. I really doubt that he would commit a murder!
- Promises are to keep. Unfortunately, I can't keep this one, missis Marge.

46

Marge remained silent and Herbie left the apartment with Albert. When they got into the car, Herbie started thinking and Albert asked.

- What are we going to do now, mister Fox?

Herbie looked at Albert and replied.

- I'm thinking, mister Fringe. Needless to say, I suppose that Daniel is on thin ice already.
- Do you think he's the murderer?
- On one hand, something tells me that he is. On the other one, I don't think so. Even if the testimonies would fit together some pieces towards him, it still just doesn't make sense very much. Why would he put a daisy next to his body? Would he be able to murder a friend who was with him in the bar that same night? Would it be worth a few pieces of diamonds? Either someone lied to us about something or we're missing a lot of information.
- Do you want interrogate Frank's mother?
- I'm thinking about that. She may give us some insights, so I suggest doing that.
- And what about Marge? Are you suspicious about her as well?
- Of course. She might be involved in those diamonds even more than Daniel. Still, I trust her more than I trust Daniel. Anyway, don't worry about it. We're here to solve this murder.

VII.

Elizabeth Lombardo
4 March 1947

After a moment of silence, Herbie spoke again.

- I'm very tired. I think that we are still able to go and visit Elizabeth Lombardo, though. You know what? Let's go to the Black Dragon restaurant, which is just two blocks away from here. I'm starving! Who's supposed to make it through the entire day without food?
- All right, mister Fox. I'm quite hungry myself.

Albert drove to the restaurant. They both entered and sat at the table. After a few seconds, a waiter came to their table and asked.

- What would you like to order, gentlemen?

Herbie replied in a dry manner with a menu in his hands.

- This steak looks decent. I think I'll have it. What about you, mister Fringe?
- I'm a vegetarian. I'll have a salad.

The waiter wrote down the order and left with a statement.

- All right, gentlemen.

Herbie looked at Albert with a smile and noted.

-   You're a youngster, mister Fringe. You need to eat
    meat. In this modern world, you won't even survive
    without it. What made you decide to be a vegetarian?
-   I just don't think that animals deserve to die for food.

Herbie gave a surprised look and said.

-   That's very interesting, mister Fringe! Even though
    you chose to be a detective and explore deceased
    human bodies, you pity dead animals. Let me tell you
    something, mister Fringe. In order to be a successful
    detective, you need to have a colder attitude!

Twenty minutes had passed. Herbie became slightly nervous
and was starting to be impatient. It changed when he saw the
waiter with plates in his hands going in their direction.

-   Here you are, gentlemen. Enjoy your meal.

Herbie thanked the waiter. A few more minutes passed and
a mysterious man entered the restaurant. He wore a hat and
a brown suit. He had a round face shape with a dense
moustache above his lips. When he sat at the table, Herbie
couldn't take his eyes off him. He told Albert.

-   Do you see that man? The one wearing a brown suit,
    I think I sent him to jail once for robbing houses. It
    was in 1927. I'm not that sure, though.

50

Albert got curious and looked at him. When the man noticed that he caught the attention of both of them, he got stressed. Herbie asked the waiter for a glass of water and stated.

- I don't like this, mister Fringe. He's behaving quite strangely.
- He probably remembers you, mister Fox.
- Either that or he's onto something again.

Herbie continued eating and when he finished his steak, he decided to go and speak to the man. As he was approaching him, the man stood up in horror and started to run. He quickly got into his car and fled in high speed. Herbie shouted.

- Fringe! Fringe! Quickly! Get in the car and step on it!

Albert stood up and they both ran to the car. Herbie got very nervous.

- Step on it! He's running away, mister Fringe!

Albert accelerated quickly and chased after the man. Herbie took the transmitter and announced.

- Detective Fox, badge number 107, do you copy?

A few seconds later, a voice of a man spoke.

- Yes, copy!

Herbie continued.

- We need backup on Lincoln Avenue! There is a reckless driver heading to the highway!
- Roger that! Sending backup to Lincoln Avenue!

After a half a minute, the man hit a tree and tried to get out of the car. Herbie quickly opened the door and ran to the vehicle with a gun. He shouted.

- Get out of your vehicle! Put your hands up!

The man got out of his car and obeyed Herbie. Herbie shouted with anger.

- Who the hell are you?

The man didn't say a word and he had a determined look on his face. Herbie was trying to persuade him to speak.

- Why did you run away from us? Are you involved in a crime?

The man remained silent. Herbie chose to appear even tougher.

- If you choose to remain silent, we will arrest you and bring you in for questioning! The choice is yours!

The man resisted and looked at Herbie. He started speaking with a calm voice.

- I'm... My name is Charlie.

- Charlie who?
- Charlie Crown.

Herbie experienced a flashback. He recognized his name because he wrote it down once into his notebook. He couldn't remember the reason, though. Charlie continued.

- When I saw you in the restaurant, I recognized you. I was near the Lopez Hills Bar when you were investigating the crime scene. I got scared and I ran away.

Herbie thought of his words but he couldn't clearly understand Charlie Crown's point.

- But why did you get so terrified? Your reaction was inadequate!

Charlie tried to explain his behavior further but he still didn't make a clear point to Herbie.

- You need to understand. I have social disorders and I can get panic attacks very easily when there is something going on, which involves me at least a little bit. I'm also going to therapy for this.

Herbie got angry again.

- That doesn't give you any reason to run away from the police! Tell me, how much are you involved in the murder of Frank Lombardo?

Charlie got terrified once again and replied.

- I'm not! I'm just a caretaker in the apartment in which he lived in! Nothing else! I swear!

Herbie remembered the letter, which contained Charlie Crown's signature. Meanwhile, the police backup arrived. Herbie commanded to them.

- Bring him to the station! I want to question him more.

The police took Charlie. He was showing horror throughout the entire process. Albert got out of the car and came to Herbie.

- Who was that, mister Fox?
- The caretaker from Frank Lombardo's apartment.
- Why did he run away from us?
- He told me he had some a social disorder. There's something wrong here. I don't think he told the truth. There must be something more.
- What are we going to do now?
- We're going to visit Frank Lombardo's mother first. Then we'll go interrogate him.

They both got to the car and headed to Elizabeth Lombardo's house. When they arrived, a short, old woman opened the door. She could be around seventy-six. She had hearing problems and couldn't walk properly. She had tears in her eyes.

- Can I help you, gentlemen?
- Detective Herbie Fox. This is my detective partner, Albert Fringe. We would like to ask you a few questions about your son.
- Come in.

Elizabeth let them in. It was a small house with a narrow corridor at the entrance, which led to the living room. When they entered the living room, Elizabeth fetched a jar of tea and three mugs.

- Have yourself a treat, gentlemen.

Herbie took a cup and slowly started to drink. He thanked Elizabeth when he drank about half of it. Elizabeth sat down, too. Afterwards, as always, Herbie lead the conversation and Albert was listening. Elizabeth stated at first.

- I hope you'll catch that monster. He deserves to be hanged!
- We are not too far from it, missis Lombardo. We have three suspects already.

Elizabeth gazed at Herbie and said.

- Tell me who those people are.
- I shouldn't say that, missis Lombardo. There are no clear conclusions yet.

Elizabeth replied with anger.

- My poor son is dead! I think I deserve to be informed who might have caused his death! What a spoiled world we're living in these days!
- Believe me, missis Lombardo. I would have told you those names. If someone deserves to hear them, it's you. But we may blame someone who has nothing to do with your son's murder eventually.
- Tell me anyway, detective.

Herbie hesitated at first but he started to give hints to missis Lombardo about the suspects.

- Does the name Daniel Greg say anything to you, missis Lombardo?

Elizabeth gave a surprised look.

- Of course I do. He's the brother of my son's girlfriend. Well, ex-girlfriend already, unfortunately. Are you saying he might be the murderer?
- Actually, I'm suspicious about him primarily because he was with Frank that night.

Herbie knew he was lying. He just wanted Elizabeth to remain calm and not do anything reckless. That's why he kept the fact of Daniel being the biggest suspect a secret.

- Don't you have any evidence against him? Oh my, even detectives can't do their job properly these days!

Although Herbie got a little angry after hearing these words, he tried to remain gentle. He calmed himself down with a thought that those words had come from a senile old woman.

- Don't be so cynical, missis Lombardo. You don't even know how mentally and physically difficult our work is.
- What have I done that I ended up in this dishonest town of America?
- Let's get to the point, missis Lombardo. Mister Fringe, pay close attention.

Herbie put his mug on the table and started the interrogation. Albert took the notebook and wrote down notes.

- What can you tell us about your son?
- What do you want to know? It's not clear to me.
- Describe him in detail. Tell me everything you can about his personality.

Elizabeth's eyes started to get moist again.

- My son... He was a good man. He was a loving son and he was honest.

Elizabeth took a handkerchief and wiped her tears. After a little while, she continued.

- His personality was unique. He wasn't the same as the other men. He was a great student in school and he liked to help people. And yes, even he had some issues. Who doesn't, mister Fox?

Herbie continued with a bit more sensitive voice from this point.

- Of course, missis Lombardo. Could you define what you mean by saying that his personality was unique?
- I can't describe it clearly. He was just different. He saw the world in a very particular way of his.
- Could you tell me about your son's past?
- He was a very good boy and son, but sometimes he easily got in trouble. He had some mood swings in which he made his temper apparent. I remember that he fought a boy because of a girl once. He was just strange. He also hung out with the wrong people.
- What people?
- All kinds of bad people. It was either someone who didn't have his mind in the right place or someone even worse, a criminal. I remember that when he was a teenager, I found a small bag of marijuana in his pants. I immediately forbad him to see those people who gave it to him.

Herbie got surprised and asked.

- Do you want to tell me that Frank had some bad connections?
- It was a long time ago. I doubt that he had some connections like that before his death.
- Did your son ever have some problems with law?
- He sometimes hung out with those wrong people and did some silly things. When he got into some trouble, I really think it wasn't because of his own will. There wasn't a single day when the police didn't knock on our door. I can only hope that he didn't have any problems that I didn't know about. He kept everything bad to himself and never told me about the things he wasn't proud of.
- I think I know what you mean by that, missis Lombardo. Can you tell us something about the diamonds?

Elizabeth thought for a moment and replied.

- Wait for a moment, detective. Something's coming up in my mind. I think he mentioned it. It was about how he had an argument with his girlfriend's brother.
- That's all right, missis Lombardo. You don't have to tell us about that. We have enough information from the previous witnesses. What can you tell us about the relationship between Frank and Marge?
- Assuming from what I saw, they looked happy. I would pick someone else for him, though. I don't really like her type of women. She's just too easy-

going. But I was glad that he could find someone after his divorce.
-   He was married?
-   Yes, he was. Bernadette Moon was his wife.
-   What was the reason of their divorce?
-   To tell the truth, I don't even know myself. I think they didn't get along with each other anymore. I'm even wondering how they fell in love at that time. They were quite opposite to each other.
-   Do you have grandchildren, missis Lombardo?
-   That's a good question, detective! Do you see any pictures of children in my house? No, I don't. Bernadette even wanted to have children, but Frank didn't. Look at me now! My one and only son is dead and I don't have any grandchildren! Not to mention that I'm a widow. I'm about to die soon, too. This is not how I thought it would be.

Elizabeth got into even deeper sadness.

-   How long has it been since your son's divorce?
-   It's been a few years.

Herbie saw that Elizabeth couldn't handle the conversation anymore. He decided to end the interrogation.

-   All right, missis Lombardo. I don't want to make you suffer any longer. If you think of anything else, call me. This is my card. You're the only person who hasn't told me a single lie and who won't throw the card into the trash.

Herbie put his card on the table and quietly left with Albert. When he was at the door, he added.

- Take care of yourself, missis Lombardo. You're a very strong woman. I believe that things can be good in your life.

Herbie and Albert left. Herbie was slightly depressed after the conversation with Elizabeth and asked.

- What's the time, mister Fringe?

Albert looked at his watch.

- It's quarter past four, mister Fox.

Herbie thought for a while and said.

- I'm not sure, mister Fringe. I think we should continue tomorrow. We've been through a lot today. I bet that you agree with me.
- You're right, mister Fox. My family is waiting for me at home.
- You're a father, mister Fringe? That's impressive! How old are your children?
- I have a five-year-old son and a two-year-old daughter.
- That's wonderful, mister Fringe. You're a true man!

- What about you, mister Fox? Do you have children?
- I have three. They're all adults now. Two sons and a daughter. My firstborn son went to Europe and I haven't seen him for years now. How I wish we would get along better. My second son is now studying law. I think he wants to follow my footsteps. He deserves an easier job than I have, I would say. My daughter got married a few months ago. I'm so proud of her. She's a surgeon.
- How old are they, mister Fox?

Herbie smiled.

- I don't want to appear witty, mister Fringe. They're not much younger than you are. Back in the day, it was quite different with the youngsters.

Albert laughed and continued.

- And what about your wife, mister Fox?
- Well, unfortunately, she passed away. She died of a lung cancer. I'll never forget her. Sometimes, I can still see her and hear her.

Herbie's mood got lower again. After a while, he added.

- All right, mister Fringe. See you at the station tomorrow. Remember, a terrified racy caretaker is awaiting us. We also need to investigate Frank Lombardo's flat. I'll research all of our investigations and evidence tonight. You can do the same if you want to, mister Fringe.

After these words, they both said goodbye to each other. Herbie came home and changed his clothes. Wearing only a flat top afterwards, he put a piece of sausage on the table. After a while, he cut slices of bread and started eating. He was glad that he was finally home. Interrogations were very exhausting for him. Three hours passed and Herbie was still thinking about the case. He went by his plan and put all the evidence on the table. The night was increasing and the storm appeared. Herbie sat down and started analyzing the clues. He grabbed the piece of daisy and thought to himself.

- Why did the murderer place this daisy next to the body? Was he trying to say something? Does it symbolize something? Or is it just a sick custom of his? Also, it's artificial. It may have something hidden on it somewhere.

Herbie observed the piece of daisy in detail. He couldn't find anything until he saw something peculiar on one of the petals. He looked for a magnifying glass and tried to concentrate on it. He saw a small-embossed number one.

- Number one? What's that supposed to mean? Is it his first victim? Does it mean that we can expect him to strike again?

He didn't see anything else on the piece of daisy. He carried on to the next evidence. It was the letter from the caretaker. He observed the envelope. He found it to be strange that the caretaker wrote the address of the apartment twice. It looked like he sent the letter through the post office, but there wasn't any stamp. Herbie couldn't see the reason why the caretaker felt the need to write down the address twice. He opened up the envelope and started to read the letter. It was written with a blue inked pen.

Waena Apartments
1320 Aala Street Honolulu, HI 96817
(866) 423-9317

Dear mister Lombardo.

I went through the rent payments for the month of February and I have some news for you. Yes, once again, with regret and anger, I inform you that you're the only person in this apartment who hasn't paid the rent. The deadline of the payment was set for the 28 February 1947. It's been almost a week since this date has passed. Could you explain to me, why didn't you pay the rent again? I gave you a clear warning that I can throw you out of your apartment after three late payments. This is, as you may know, the fourth time. Do you realize this fact, mister Lombardo? You can be glad that I'm so generous towards you. I moved your deadline to the end of this week. If I don't receive your payment, you can pack your bags and move out. I'm not willing to tolerate your manners anymore! Not only that, but

I have also received complaints about you from the neighbors. This is your last warning! I repeat, one last warning!

With regards,

Charlie Crown (the caretaker).

Herbie put down the letter and noticed a small piece of folded paper in the envelope. He unfolded it and number one was written on it with thick large-sized writing. Herbie thought with the piece of paper in his hands.

- Number one again? Why does it appear on the piece of daisy AND in his envelope to Lombardo? Is Charlie Crown the murderer? I wonder how he'll explain not only this fact but also how he was able to almost blackmail Lombardo when he has social problems. It doesn't make sense to me. Would a caretaker murder someone because of late payments? I would have to work overtime if each caretaker thought like that! But also, why would Daniel murder his good friend? Because of some pieces of diamonds? Does Charlie Crown know anything about the diamonds? Maybe he has some intentions with them and he's trying to cover up himself with telling everyone he has disorders. And what about Marge? I can't think of any reason why she would do that but... And generally, what the hell does Frank Lombardo has to do with those diamonds? It's simply a thing of the Greg family. There's not much left after Frank, obviously.

Herbie thought of the card of Malfred Ash, which he had in his coat pocket.

- I almost forgot. I need to take a look whether I still have that card of the guy named Ash. He thought, I think I wrote it down to my notebook.

Herbie opened his notebook and saw Malfred Ash's address on one page.

- I have an idea. I'll try to find Malfred Ash in the yellow pages and call it. Just to see what comes up when you call his number.

Herbie looked for the yellow pages. He found it on a shelf after a while. He searched for Malfred Ash and after a few minutes, he found his number. He dialed the number. When he dialed it for the first time, noone answered. When he dialed it for the second time, voice of a woman spoke.

- Hello?
- Good evening, miss. Is this the number of Malfred Ash?

After a moment of silence, the woman replied with insecurity.

- Who's calling?
- Herbie Fox. Could I speak to him, please?

Another moment of silence occurred. This time, Herbie could hear a whispering. A short while later, Herbie asked.

- Are you there, miss?

The whispering went on and Herbie raised his voice.

- I advise you to answer me, miss! I'm starting to lose my patience!

Herbie could hear a conversation between some man and the woman from the telephone, but he didn't get any answer. The woman hung up. Herbie thought to himself.

- Something's wrong here! I'll try to call it once again twenty minutes later. I won't go easy on them!

Twenty minutes had passed and Herbie tried to call the number again. This time, a deep man voice spoke. There was a loud music playing in the background and many other voices. Herbie didn't want to say that he was a detective.

- Hello?
- Good evening. Is this the number of Malfred Ash?
- Who's asking?
- Herbie Fox.
- Who?
- Never mind. Listen, I found your card somewhere and I wanted to ask whether you offer some services.
- Well, yes. I'm an electrician. I repair household appliances.

- Are you treating all of your customers like this?
- Look, I'm busy. Do you want something from me or not?

Herbie hung up. He found it unnecessary to argue with some arrogant stranger.

- An electrician? Huh... I don't believe that for some reason! Why would Frank Lombardo have a card of an electrician in his pocket? He was an electrician, too! Were they co-workers? But still, why would Lombardo need his card? That's a question that Malfred Ash needs to answer tomorrow. Should I even go as a detective? It would maybe be better if I dressed as a civilian. What can this guy have to do with the case? Electrician? I doubt so!

Herbie yawned and thought to himself.

- I'm really tired. I've had enough. I should go to bed. Who knows if I might solve this weird murder?

Herbie brushed his teeth, put on his pajamas, and went to bed. After a little while, he fell asleep.

VIII.

Charlie Crown

The Police Station
5 March 1947

It was another sunny morning and Herbie met Albert at the police station. They went to the Lieutenant's office. The lieutenant asked.

- How are you doing so far? Is there any progress?

Herbie started talking.

- We're working on it. We have several suspects. I think we might solve the case today. We still need to interrogate some people and investigate some places though.
- Should I consider it to be good news, mister Fox?
- I think you won't regret doing that, lieutenant.
- That's good, mister Fox. The journalists arranged a press conference today. They want to hear only positive statements! They are like leeches, but it's understandable that they want to put out something interesting.
- Don't worry, lieutenant. We have it under the control.
- Good! Have you found out the motive yet?
- There are misunderstandings around some diamonds. That's why I think it may be a material motive. Either

that or we still don't know something about Frank Lombardo.

- And what about that piece of daisy? I bet that those leeches will ask me about that.
- It's probably a custom of the murderer. I haven't found out yet. All I have are assumptions and I wouldn't say them out loud if I were you.
- All right, so it's his custom. That should be all, mister Fox. I think I might be able to handle it from this point. I'm sure that a detective like you will catch the murderer as soon as he shows up. You can both leave now. Take care.
- Goodbye.

Herbie and Albert left. As they were walking through the corridor, Officer Blake stopped them.

- Fox! Haven't you forgot about Charlie Crown yesterday? He was sitting in the interrogation room for hours and you haven't showed up!
- Really? I may need help with some things. What did you do with him?
- We locked him up in the cell after three hours. Poor guy, he was so confused about what was happening.

They all three laughed out loud. Herbie got a little upset about it and said.

70

- That's all right, mister Blake. He can thank you for informing us about that. We're going to interrogate him. In which room is he in?
- I'm going to tell the guards. He's still in the cell so you need to wait for about ten minutes. We'll put him in the room two. This time, it would be nice of you to show up, mister Fox!
- Thank you, mister Blake. I would be lost without you!
- A pack of Pall Mall should be enough to show your gratitude, mister Fox. I think I deserve it after what I've done for you. Don't worry, I'll share it with you and we'll both have a nice smoke after work.
- Of course, mister Blake. I just need to solve this case first.
- All right, wait here then.

Herbie and Albert sat down and after a moment, Dean Marston appeared and came to them.

- Mister Fox! Mister Fox! Can I ask you about the investigation?
- We're making some progress, mister Marston. We have no clear conclusions yet. What about you? Have you found out something new?
- No, I haven't. Do you have some new suspects?
- I wouldn't say that there is someone as suspicious as Daniel Greg, but yes, we do. Basically, everyone who had something to do with Frank Lombardo is a suspect.

- That's certain, mister Fox. Anyway, I have a lot of work to do today. I was just curious about the case. I'm going to leave you now. See you around, mister Fox.
- See you around, mister Marston.

Marston went away. Herbie started talking with Albert.

- Mister Fringe, I haven't heard anything from you for a while. What do you think about the investigation so far?
- I don't have much to say, mister Fox. I have mixed feelings about everything that occurred yesterday. I even wonder if I chose the right job.
- This is your first homicide case, mister Fringe. You'll get used to the pressure as time passes. You don't even know how much pressure I'm under right now! I can tell you that being a detective's partner is one of the softest jobs you can have on the squad! Have you got some thoughts about this case to add?
- I've thought about the evidence quite intensively yesterday, but I couldn't come up with anything. What about you, mister Fox?
- I do have some new information. I've observed the letter from the caretaker. I've also tried to call Malfred Ash but it wasn't successful. Lombardo had his card in his coat pocket. First time when I called, a woman answered the phone. She ignored me almost the entire time. It took a few minutes before

I got to talk with Ash himself. Let me tell you. You won't find so easily such a talkative electrician like he is! Thinking about it, we need to visit him today. I'm just wondering whether it would be more effective to come as a civilian. I don't like what was happening during our phone calls.

- That won't be necessary, in my opinion. If he really keeps something a secret from us, he will probably try to run away.
- That's not what I'm pointing at. He might lie to us the entire time. In a way, you're right. When he does, we'll be able to send him behind the prison bars.

Ten minutes passed and officer Blake came back.

- He's waiting for you, mister Fox. Be careful, though. He looks angry. You probably have to go tough on him!
- Thank you, Officer Blake.

Herbie and Albert stood up and went to the interrogation room number two. Charlie Crown was sitting at the table already. He had a furious look on his face. Herbie sat down and started the interrogation. As usual, Albert was transcribing.

- Greetings, mister Crown. We meet again.

Charlie Crown replied with fury.

- Greetings, mister Fox. I'm so grateful that you put me in a cell for no reason! I've enjoyed staying the night here!
- I'm glad to hear that, mister Crown. At least I don't need to have any regrets about what happened.
- Do you understand the word irony, detective?
- Of course I do, mister Crown. I would have asked you the same question because you probably didn't understand me correctly.
- I'm happy that you even showed up, detective. It was so sad for me to be here alone.
- Excuse me. Is this the same Charlie Crown who I met yesterday? Because I observe quite a big change in your behavior, mister Crown! You're being rude to the detective! What happened to the Charlie Crown who ran away from me and then tried to explain me his social phobias with fear? You're a very complicated person!
- You're hilarious, detective! Just try to go against me! I have official documents from my shrink. I'll sue you and I'll be so kind that I won't mention my night spent here does that sound allright to you?
- Oh, stop it, mister Crown! Do you want me to go against you? Well, I have something to show you then!

Herbie took Charlie's letter to Frank from his pocket. He unfolded it and he held it firmly in his hands, pointing towards Charlie Crown.

74

- See this, mister Crown? You have a nice handwriting. You deserve a new luxury pen. You also have a lot of courage! Just one thing, I wouldn't expect it from someone who ran away from us yesterday. You literally threatened Frank. You said you'll make him homeless!

Charlie defended himself.

- I had a right to do that! That man was nothing, but trouble! He never paid the rent on time and he caused some other problems, too. I'm glad that scum died! People like him have no place in this world!
- Be careful, mister Crown! Nobody deserves to die. It doesn't matter whom we're talking about. Everybody deserves to live! Anyway, you're a new suspect in this case.
- Excuse me? How dare you? Do you know who I am? I studied law! I wanted to work as an advocate!
- I don't care, mister Crown! I don't judge people by their education or job! I have no idea who you might be and I'm not even interested, to be honest. Now, tell me. Do you know something about the diamonds?
- I have no idea what you're talking about.
- Be honest, mister Crown!
- I seriously don't know.
- All right, I believe you then. But what does this mean?

Herbie showed Charlie the small piece of paper with number one written on it.

- What's not to understand, mister Fox? In our apartment, we number the alerts. Not all of them, only serious ones. Alert about the late payment is one of them. Lombardo could be glad that my previous warnings were only informal. Since this was his first formal warning, I needed to put this piece of paper into the envelope. Ridiculous, I know, but that's how it works in our apartment.
- That's interesting, mister Crown! Could you explain why the number one was written on the piece of daisy, as well?
- No, I can't.
- Well, all right then, mister Crown. One last question. Do you have keys to Lombardo's apartment?
- Of course I do. What kind of a caretaker would I be if I didn't?
- Isn't that illegal, mister Crown?
- No, it's not! I respect the privacy of everyone in the apartment. Even if you probably don't think so.
- I'm not accusing you of anything, mister Crown. We just need the keys from Lombardo's apartment, that's all. If you give them to us, you are free for now. I'm saying that because if I had to judge purely by this interrogation, I would send you to prison right away!
- How rude! That's unbelievable! You can be glad if I give you the keys!

- Either that or you'll spend some more cruel nights here until you're claimed to be innocent!
- Come with me to the apartment.

The guard asked Herbie.

- Are you leaving, mister Fox?
- Yes. You can free him.
- Goodbye, mister Fox.
- Goodbye.

Herbie and Albert stood up and left with Charlie. When they opened the door, Herbie told Charlie.

- No need to drive, mister Crown! You're coming with us.

They all three got in the car. During the commute, Herbie talked with Charlie.

- Where is my car, mister Fox?
- That's not important right now, mister Crown. I need to have you near me all the time!
- How rude!
- I feel the same, mister Crown. You're behaving inappropriately towards us!
- Inappropriately? Should I polish your shoes, detective?
- That's a good offer. A better attitude would be a better one though.

- You don't even deserve it, detective!
- Do you know what, mister Crown? Just be quiet from now on. I think we'll be both glad when you don't end up in prison for good.

IX.

Apartment of Frank Lombardo
5 March 1947

Charlie stopped talking. He hadn't said a word until they got there. After a few minutes, they arrived at the apartment. Charlie Crown led Herbie and Albert to his flat where he had Frank's keys. He had a big board in his workroom, which contained copies of keys of all the people in the apartment. He grabbed keys to Lombardo's flat and gave them to Herbie.

- Get out of my sight, detective. You have to return them afterwards. The person who will rent Frank Lombardo's apartment will need a copy of these keys.
- Don't you worry, mister Crown. I don't think I'll stop by anytime soon at this apartment.
- Please, just leave.

Herbie and Albert left Charlie Crown's flat. They looked around the apartment and soon afterwards found Frank Lombardo's flat. Herbie gave the keys to Albert and said.

- Would you be so kind, mister Fringe?

Albert opened the door and they both entered. There was a strong smell and mess everywhere.

- It looks like that window hasn't been opened for days. We have to do something about that terrifying smell!

Albert stated.

- I'll open the window up in the living room.
- Walk through the entire flat and observe everything that might be interesting, mister Fringe.
- Can I touch those things?
- It shouldn't be a problem but I would recommend you to wear gloves. I always carry one pair in my pocket. Just in case.

Herbie took a pair of gloves out of his coat pocket and gave it to Albert.

- Here you are. I'll grab a napkin. Either way, fingerprints won't really help us.
- All right, mister Fox. Thank you.
- Go through the living room. I'll check the Lombardo's workroom.
- All right, mister Fox.
- If you see anything really interesting, call me. I'll also tell you about my findings.

Albert nodded his head. He put on the white gloves and went to the living room. Herbie took off to the workroom. He opened the door and entered.

- Let's see. A big dirty room with a table. Plenty of stuff lying on the floor. I don't think that Lombardo was a very tidy person. I wouldn't be able to work in a room like this one.

Herbie looked around more and he saw tiny papers on the floor. Most of them were some documents, but one piece of paper interested him. It was tickets from a cash machine with a word *LOSE* written on it. He noticed more losing tickets soon afterwards.

- It's obvious that Frank had a gambling problem. He lost his money and couldn't pay the rent on time because of it. But how did he get the money eventually?

Herbie looked further and sat at the table. He observed each paper that was on the table. There were documents, utility bills, game tickets, telephone, and a typewriter. Herbie noticed one flyer. It was an advertisement of a jewelry store on the Lincoln Avenue. On the back of the flyer, there was a jewelry auction advertisement.

- Did Lombardo have some intentions with the diamonds eventually? It wasn't his property.

After a little while, he noticed a letter from Daniel Greg on the table. He started reading it.

Frank,

Don't do anything irrational with the money I lent you to pay the rent. You have enough problems already! You need to stop with the gambling. Your chances of winning are very slim, anyway. If you spend my money on the game tickets,

I'll never lend you again! Don't tell Marge, but I found buyers for the diamonds. They offered me two million dollars for them. Can you believe that? Soon, I'll be a millionaire! All you have to do is to sign those papers I gave you earlier. You know about that statement in my mother's will. Since you're my future brother-in-law already, you can give me all the rights for the ownership of the diamonds. Dealing with Marge would be a lot more difficult. I hope that you'll be the wise one and that you will help me. We'll go 50/50 with the money. Can you even imagine what you can buy with that kind of money? See you on Friday. Pick me up at six.

Daniel

-    What have we got here? Not only did Daniel want the diamonds for selling purposes, but he also wanted to betray his sister! I suppose that Frank didn't agree with signing the contract. I can easily imagine the reason why he could murder Lombardo. He wanted permission, which he didn't receive. With the murder of Lombardo, not only would he be able to find another way to the diamonds, but also, he wouldn't have to share his money with anyone. That makes sense but it still does not look like the full story. I'll look further. Greg is on a thin ice, though. If I find evidence that tells about some connections with mafia, I'll arrest him immediately!

82

Herbie looked through the papers further. There were many letters. One of them caught his interest. On the envelope, there was only Frank's address and no signature or name of the sender.

Lombardo,

Boss wants to meet you and talk about some things. Come on Wednesday to the Riviera Bar at six o'clock. Come alone.

- I have a feeling that Lombardo wasn't a saint, either. It looks like a letter from some mafia!

Herbie stood up and continued searching for objects and he found a magazine about gardening. There was an illustration of daisy placed on a diamond on the front cover. Inside the magazine, there was Frank's order for subscription of the magazine for the year 1948.

- Lombardo and gardening? He can't even take care of his flat! Besides, there's no garden nearby! Is it possible that the murderer burglarized into Lombardo's flat before he committed the murder? It would probably explain the mess that's all around here, too. I think it's time to call to the Riviera Bar. I guess that poor Frank won't mind if I use his telephone. That cover is so ironical!

Herbie looked for a phonebook. He found one in the drawer of the table. He searched for the Riviera Bar's phone number and dialed it. A male barkeeper answered the phone.

- Hello?
- Good afternoon, sir. Detective Herbie Fox speaking. Can we talk?
- Yeah, we can.
- I have a few questions. Does the name Frank Lombardo say anything to you?
- I'll be honest with you, no. But I think I heard the name Lombardo in this bar a few times. Are you investigating his murder? I've heard about it on the radio.
- Yes, I do. Listen, you need to remember as much as you can. Have you seen a group of men with a man who was alone?
- A group of men? I can see that every night here, pal. But as a matter of fact, I have. Their table was the one from which I heard the name Lombardo.
- Do you know what they were talking about?
- They were mentioning some debts. At one moment, they were talking about game tickets. At the other one, they were talking about utility bills. I remember that because they were talking loudly.
- Do you remember anything more?
- They all left together at about nine. That's all I can tell you.
- Thank you for cooperation, mister...

- Mickens.
- Thank you for cooperation, mister Mickens. You have helped us with this information.
- Do me a favor, detective. Catch that smug who committed the murder and make him pay!
- Don't worry about that, mister Mickens. Bye.
- Bye.

Herbie wrote down all the information he heard to his notebook. When he finished, Albert called him to the living room.

- Mister Fox! Come here!

Herbie stood up and quickly went to Albert. He had an open box in his hands.

- Have you found something, mister Fringe?
- Look! In this box, there was a set of knives, which look similar to the one we found! It even looks like that exact size and shape is missing!
- So my thoughts are true! The murderer did break into this flat before the murder! He searched the entire flat and then took a knife with which he decided to commit the murder! It all makes sense!
- One question. Why are there no signs of violent entrance on either the doors or the windows?
- That's a thoughtful question. Either the murderer owned the key to this flat or he had some serious skills with a lock pick. We only know about one

person who owned the keys to this flat and that is Charlie Crown. I would say that it's improbable that Daniel Greg had the keys, but nothing is impossible!

- What now? Have you found something?
- I've found some interesting letters and a bunch of game tickets. I've even called to the Riviera Bar. It was because Lombardo got a letter to meet there. There was no sign of a sender anywhere. One thing remains, though. Lombardo did go to that bar and he knew the person who called him there! It looks like gambling had an important role in Lombardo's life.
- So what are we going to do?
- I'm thinking. Do you have any ideas, mister Fringe?
- Is it possible to find out something about the person who sent that letter?
- That letter was written on a typewriter. That means we don't have a lot of options. It would be very difficult to identify that person based on the writing. In order to do that, we would have to research all the typewriter models. They all have almost the same type of writing. The only differences are on some particular letters. We don't have enough time for that!
- What about going to the Riviera Bar?
- That's unnecessary. I've spoken to the barkeeper already. We have all the information from that place. Interesting fact is that Lombardo left with those people in the bar. Who knows what for, right? They could have gone gambling. One thing just came into

my mind. What about that Ash guy? Should we do the typical interrogation or act as civilians? We need to come up with a reason why we're visiting him in that case.

- I think we should just proceed usually.
- You're right, mister Fringe. Do you think that there could be anything more in this flat?
- I don't know. Either way, I don't think so.

They both researched the whole flat again. When they couldn't find anything, they left, and got in the car. Herbie took a card of Malfred Ash and gave it to Albert.

- Let's go, then. Do you know where his apartment is located?
- I'll probably need to take a look around, but I do.
- Step on it, mister Fringe!

X.

Malfred Ash
5 March 1947

Approximately fifteen minutes had passed and they arrived at the apartment. They found out that Malfred Ash lived on the third story. When they reached the door and knocked, noone opened. Herbie had heard some noise coming out of that door but he wasn't sure.

- It seems like something happened last night, mister Fringe.

After a while, Herbie lost his patience and decided to do something.

- I've had enough! Step out, mister Fringe! I'm going to make some noise!
- What do you want to do, mister Fox?

Herbie made two steps back and kicked out the door with strong force.

- If it's impossible with the good way, it's possible with the bad way! Come on in!

They both entered the flat and looked around. The phone started ringing and Herbie answered. The caller was a man.

- Hello?
- Is it you, Malfred? You sound different somehow. Are you ill?
- Yes, I am. What do you want?
- How's... the thing? Do you have those diamonds?
- Excuse me?
- Don't you know already? Those diamonds! Boss wants to do the barter already. Those Russians are impatient so you need to act quickly or we're all going to die! So, do you have them?
- I'll call you up later.

Herbie slowly hung up and stated.

- We have the murderer, mister Fringe! Quickly, we need to find some evidence here and arrest him! Now! We don't have much time!

They both started to quickly research Malfred's flat. Albert found a box full of artificial daisies. He showed it to Herbie who shouted afterwards.

- Quickly, grab one of them!

Albert grabbed a piece of daisy and gave it to Herbie. Herbie observed it carefully and noticed the number one written on it.

- That son of a bitch! We're right! This piece of daisy is identical to the one found next to the Lombardo's body! Do you see this number one? It's exactly the same! We need more!

They continued searching. Herbie noticed Malfred's diary on the table. When he opened it, he saw a note that said **DIAMONDS – FRANK LOMBARDO** with the exact date and time when the murder occurred. Herbie stated.

- We got him! Look at this diary! See this note? It's exactly the date and time when the murder occurred!
- I see. It was very irrational to take a note of something like that.
- More! It's obvious that the reason of the murder were those diamonds. I don't know how yet, but it's true! Let's look further!

Herbie flicked through the other pages of Malfred's diary and he found Charlie Crown's phone number, as well as Daniel Greg's. Afterwards, he opened a drawer and there were keys with a tag **DIAMONDS** on them.

- It all makes sense! Charlie Crown made and gave a copy of the keys to the Lombardo's flat! Ash simply went to the flat when Lombardo wasn't at home and looked for the diamonds. Daniel Greg probably told him that he was the person who takes care of the ownership issue and Malfred misunderstood that by thinking that Lombardo owns the diamonds himself! Now, when Malfred didn't find the diamonds in Lombardo's flat, he took one of his knives and went to murder him! He probably noticed the magazine and left one of his artificial pieces next to the Lombardo's dead body. How awful! I suppose that Malfred Ash was the buyer mentioned in Daniel Greg's letter to Lombardo. Either way, Daniel Greg and Charlie Crown are getting charged as associates! Daniel doesn't even know how much he's involved in a murder of his friend. All right, mister Fringe. Let's go to the station! We don't know what Malfred Ash looks like so we can't catch him on our own.

They both left the flat and and as they were walking down the stairs, they saw a man in a green suit. He wore a hat and glasses. He had a thin figure. Herbie asked him.

- Malfred Ash?

The man looked at the detectives with horror and ran away by his car. Herbie and Albert quickly followed and chased him. Herbie spoke to the transmitter.

- This is Detective Fox, badge number 107. I need immediate backup on the Saint King Street! We're chasing the murderer of the Frank Lombardo case and he's heading towards the McCully Street! Be quick, the murderer can't escape! Do you copy?
- Roger that! Sending backup to the McCully Street!

After a few minutes of furious chase, Malfred Ash, with the help of backup, pulled over. Herbie quickly got out of the car and went to Malfred with a gun in his hands along with the other officers. Malfred Ash got out and put his hands in the air.

- Malfred Ash! You're under arrest for the murder of Frank Lombardo! You have a right to remain silent, anything you say can and will be used against in a court of law. You have the right to talk to a lawyer and have him present with you while you are being questions, if you cannot afford a lawyer, one will be appointed to you. You can decide at any time to exercise these rights and not answer any questions or make any statements. Do you understand? We have enough evidence against you! Don't even think about trying to run away again!

Herbie handcuffed Malfred and the police officers took him to the station. When they arrived, there was press all over the place already. Initially preparing for the press conference, when they saw a man in handcuffs, they all started asking questions and taking photographs.

- Do you have the murderer of Frank Lombardo?
- How did you manage to solve the case?
- What evidence do you have?
  ...

Herbie decided to be silent and ignored the questions. They both went to the lieutenant's office, while the officers were leading Malfred Ash to the prison cell. The lieutenant saw them all and asked with a smile.

- Mister Fox, once again, I'm proud of you! How did you solve the case?
- We found strong evidence in the flat of Malfred Ash and we heard a phone call intended for him. I need you to arrest Daniel Greg and Charlie Crown, too. They're associates in the murder. Their names were written down in Malfred Ash's diary!
- All right, mister Fox. I'll take care of that. So, could you explain the whole murder to me?
- Of course. The motive of the murder was a desire for pieces of diamonds and money. Diamonds were a property of missis Greg, the mother of Daniel and Marge Greg. The only connection with Lombardo around those diamonds was missis Greg's last will, which contained a very important statement for Daniel and Malfred Ash. Daniel Greg wanted to sell the diamonds but he needed permission from Frank Lombardo. He couldn't make the barter without it. I even guess that he might have planned the murder. His sister refused to give him the permission and Frank supported her by doing the same thing. The strategy of Daniel Greg may have been to murder Frank Lombardo and to emotionally abuse Marge so he can receive the permission. He received an offer for two million dollars for the diamonds. The mafia was involved. The whole case is a one large chain.

94

Daniel told Ash about the diamonds. Ash told the mafia about the diamonds. The mafia requested him soon after to commit the murder so they can do the barter. Ash's plan was simple. He thought that the diamonds are in Lombardo's flat. He requested keys from Charlie Crown, the caretaker. He was obviously a friend of Daniel Greg. Malfred wanted to take the diamonds from Lombardo's flat and do the barter as soon as possible. When he didn't find the diamonds, he decided to take a knife and murder Lombardo. Daniel Greg must have informed him about his meeting with Lombardo in the Lopez Hills Bar.

Albert added.

-   Lombardo had financial issues and he probably owed money to Malfred Ash. Debts, hazard, and diamonds caused Lombardo's death with a final act from Malfred Ash.

Herbie got surprised.

-   Excellent, mister Fringe. It looks like you've learned something!

Albert smiled and the lieutenant said.

-   Great job, detectives! Ash will be in jail for at least twenty years! The judge will decide about everything, even about the fate of Daniel Greg and Charlie

Crown. All right. Albert Fringe, I'm giving you a raise! I see that your partnership is successful and you certainly deserve it! You can go, detectives. Your work here is done!

The court sentenced Malfred Ash for fifteen years of prison. Daniel Greg got sentenced for five years of prison and Charlie Crown got sentenced for one year of community service. Marge Greg got married again a year later. She received the diamonds and they never got sold.

CHARACTERS CHARACTERISTICS

Name: Herbie Fox

Age: 60

Date of Birth: 27/2/1887

Place of Birth: Honolulu, Hawaii

Job: Detective

Family status: Widowed

Children: Philip Fox, Richard Fox, Veronica Fox-Winsley

Appearance: 5 ft 4.96 in, 209 pounds, gray hair, scar on a cheek

Name: Albert Fringe

Age: 35

Date of Birth: 30/5/1911

Place of Birth: Kailua, Hawaii

Job: Detective

Family status: Married

Children: Mark Fringe, Josephina Fringe

Appearance: 5 ft 6.93 in, 154 pounds, ginger hair, freckles

Name: Daniel Greg

Age: 42

Date of Birth: 15/8/1904

Place of Birth: California, USA

Job: Architect

Family status: In a relationship

Children: none

Appearance: 5 ft 8.9 in, 165 pounds, longer brown hair

Name: Marge Greg

Age: 40

Date of Birth: 17/1/1907

Place of Birth: California, USA

Job: Secretary

Family status: In a relationship

Children: none

Appearance: 5 ft 2.99 in, 110 pounds, blonde hair, blue eyes

Name: Frank Lombardo

Age: 41

Date of Birth: 28/2/1906

Place of Birth: Verona, Italy

Job: Postman

Family status: In a relationship

Children: none

Appearance: 5 ft 4.96 in, 154 pounds, black hair

Name: Elizabeth Lombardo

Age: 76

Date of Birth: 20/6/1870

Place of Birth: Verona, Italy

Job: Teacher (retired)

Family status: Widowed

Children: Frank Lombardo

Appearance: 4 ft 11.06 in, 132 pounds, long gray hair

Name: Malfred Ash

Age: 34

Date of Birth: 11/10/1912

Place of Birth: Honolulu, Hawaii

Job: Electrician

Family status: Single

Children: none

Appearance: 5 ft 1.81 in, 126 pounds, brown hair

Name: Robert Wintski

Age: 52

Date of Birth: 20/4/1894

Place of Birth: Kapolei, Hawaii

Job: Bartender

Family status: Married

Children: Sylvia Wintski, Thomas Wintski

Appearance: 5 ft 4.17 in, 247 pounds, short black hair

Name: Charlie Crown

Age: 43

Date of Birth: 20/12/1903

Place of Birth: Honolulu, Hawaii

Job: Caretaker

Family status: Single

Children: none

Appearance: 5 ft 6.93 in, 159 pounds, brown hair

Name: Phil More

Age: 63

Date of Birth: 25/3/1883

Place of Birth: Honolulu, Hawaii

Job: Lieutenant

Family status: Married

Children: George More

Appearance: 5 ft 4 in, 134 pounds, gray hair

Name: Angie Rothford

Age: 78

Date of Birth: 14/3/1868

Place of Birth: Kaneohe, Hawaii

Job: Saleswoman (retired)

Family status: Married

Children: Abraham Rothford

Appearance: 4 ft 12 in, 143 pounds, gray hair

Name: Thomas Blake

Age: 45

Date of Birth: 9/4/1901

Place of Birth: Minnesota, USA

Job: Police officer

Family status: Divorced

Children: Claudia Blake

Appearance: 5 ft 6 in, 165 pounds, short black hair

Name: Dean Marston

Age: 65

Date of Birth: 21/9/1881

Place of Birth: Honolulu, Hawaii

Job: Forensic analytic

Family status: Widowed

Children: none

Appearance: 5 ft 3 in, 139 pounds, hair dyed brown

Name: Andrew Shelby

Age: 38

Date of Birth: 13/5/1908

Place of Birth: Honolulu, Hawaii

Job: Police officer

Family status: Married

Children: John Shelby, Anna Shelby

Appearance: 5 ft 7 in, 174 pounds, brown hair

Name: Mike Hannigan

Age: 52

Date of Birth: 29/11/1894

Place of Birth: Berlin, Germany

Job: Doorkeeper

Family status: Single

Children: none

Appearance: 5 ft 3 in, 163 pounds, black hair

Name: Richard Mickens

Age: 42

Date of Birth: 9/1/1905

Place of Birth: Aiea, Hawaii

Job: Barkeeper

Family status: Single

Children: none

Appearance: 5 ft 8.7 in, 180 pounds, brown hair

The Mystery of Bloody River
Steven Vagovics

Some of the story information may be lacking due to their mentioning in the previous book episodes of the series.

I.

Honolulu, Hawaii
2 December, 1947

It was another sunny day on Honolulu.

Gilbert Frederich, local businessman, was on his way to work. He was a middle-aged man with brown hair, a fattish figure and green eyes who owned one of the biggest companies involved with cash loan services in Honolulu called SUNBEAM FINANCES. It was known that Gilbert was a rich man. After all, his company was making thousands of dollars in profit every day and still growing. As he was walking through Foster Botanic Garden, he saw a few young children who were on a school trip with their teacher. They spread joy all around the park and Gilbert looked at the teacher. She was an older woman with blond hair, blue eyes and a fit figure.

Gilbert started talking with her.

- Look at them little children! How much joy they're having! Isn't it just amazing?

Teacher replied with a smile on her face.

- Yes, I agree. They are my pride. I see a great potential in each one of them. It doesn't matter that they are only nine years old. I can envision the intelligent and well-behaved adults they are about to become.

Gilbert nodded his head.

- It's just fascinating how one can develop so rapidly during so little time. Suddenly, it stops and you remain almost exactly the same for so long.
- Perhaps, that's true.

After a moment of silence, the teacher realised something and asked with curiosity.

- Wait a minute. Aren't you that rich man, Gilbert? I've seen you so many times on television already!

Gilbert smiled and replied.

- Yes, that's me.

The teacher continued.

- Just a moment. I think I saw a report just this morning about you.

Suddenly, Gilbert was surprised.

- What was it about?
- It was a report about some changes that are about to happen in your company.

Gilbert was even more suprised and wondered.

- I don't know anything about it. Did they mention precisely what changes are about to happen?
- No, they didn't. At least, I don't remember anything.
- I see.

Gilbert became slightly nervous.

- I'll keep on walking then. I have to go there to find out about it. See you later.
- Bye.

Gilbert walked on through the park and couldn't think of a single reason to explain what the teacher had talked about. He started to rush. After a few minutes, he reached the company and entered. A lot of people were panicking inside the building and Gilbert was terrified. When he walked into his office, Joe Pentham appeared . It was Gilbert's business partner who ran the company with him. He was a tall person with black hair and a thin figure who was just as old as Gilbert. He asked with fear.

- Gil, have you heard the news yet?

Gilbert answered with insecurity.

- No, I haven't. What the hell happened? I don't like this. Why are so many people here?

Joe replied.

- Gil, this is serious. Do you remember that new company Calico?
- Yes, I do. They were about to go bankrupt just a few days ago. What about them?

Joe got a bit upset and explained.

-   Listen, Gil. I don't know how to tell you this but... They are taking over!

Gilbert looked at Joe with surprise. He didn't understand.

-   What do you mean they are taking over?

Joe started shouting.

-   They are taking over! Literally! They ran a huge campaign about their cash loan services which provided offers we just can't compete with! Most of our clients switched over to the them, leaving us hopeless. We're screwed!

Gilbert thought for a little.

-   Wait, something's weird here. Our clients signed a clear contract which stated their liability with us until their loan is paid off. How could they just switch to Calico? I can't accept that.
-   It's a complicated situation. They found a loophole in our contract papers and took advantage of it right away! This resulted in several benefits for people who switched. Additionally, they found a way to do it behind our backs!

Gilbert started pacing around the office nervously.

-   This is not good. Oh, this is bad! This is bad! So what's next?

- Our company is getting shut down and we're going to lose a lot of money.
- How much money are we talking about?

Joe grabbed a file and gave it to Gilbert without words.

- Take a look at this. It's all stated here. I recommend you sit down, Gil.

Gilbert sat down and opened the file. His expression turned to fury. Joe tried to calm him down.

- I'm so sorry, Gil. I know it's a lot of money but I'm sure you'll be able to handle it well.

Gilbert remained silent.

- Gil, are you all right? Is it more than you expected? Gil?

Gilbert stood up. He began to speak with anger.

- Do you... Do you really want to know?

Joe replied with worry.

- Yes, tell me.
- All right then. I'll tell you.

Gilbert grabbed a lamp which was placed on his desk and threw it at the door fiercely. The lamp smashed to pieces. Afterwards, he shouted.

- It's almost everything I've got! What the bloody hell? For goodness' sake, how could you let something like this happen? This is unbelievable!

Joe replied with fear.

- Gil, look, I'm sorry! There was basically nothing I could do about it! Even if I could do something, I don't have all the rights that you do!

Gilbert slowly sat down again and stated in a quiet, angry voice.

- Get out of my office right now. I need to be alone.
- But Gil!
- Right... now!

Joe left the office and Gilbert sat in his chair for a moment, thinking about the whole situation. After a moment, he grabbed his bag and left the building.

A few hours later, he came home where his wife was waiting for him. Her name was Claudia. She was a tall, blue-eyed woman with long black hair and a thin figure. When Gilbert opened the door, Claudia was talking on a telephone.

- What do you mean by that? Oh, I see.

Gilbert became uncomfortable when he heard these words. He thought that the conversation might have been about him. Claudia hung up the telephone and spoke to Gilbert.

- Gilbert, I've just found out about what happened today.

Gilbert got upset. Claudia continued talking.

- Look, Gilbert. It's okay. We can handle this. We still have enough money to start something new.
- I'm not sure about that, honey.
- Why not?
- Do you know how big of a loss this situation has brought to us? Calico simply took over! All of my clients are there now. I have nothing to work with because of that!
- Let's just hope we can figure this out, Gilbert.
- But how, Claudia? We have nothing! No money, no business anymore and we can probably say goodbye to this house!

Gilbert became very angry and strongly punched the wall. Claudia was shocked. After a little while, Gilbert calmed down and said.

- I need to go out. I just... can't stand here without doing anything. I'm sorry, honey.

Gilbert quickly opened the door and ran away. Claudia was trying to reason with him but without success. Gilbert was gone.

II.

Honolulu, Hawaii
3 December, 1947

The next morning, Claudia woke up and Gilbert was still not back. Full of fear, she went to the kitchen, turned on the radio, made herself a cup of coffee and sat at the table with the newspaper. The news broadcast started.

- *Good morning Honolulu. In today's newsflash – riot in Jerusalem caused by the United Nations, three women escapees from Honolulu on their visit, a man found by the river.*

Claudia was even more terrified. With a cup of coffee in her hands, she listened with the darkest images in her mind already. The news continued.

- *The riot in Jerusalem occured yesterday when the Arab Higher Committee declared a three-day strike and public protest against the United Nations plan to create two states – one Jewish and one Arab in Palestine, according to the 1947 UN Partition Plan. Our reporters have just been sent to Palestine to bring you more information about the situation. Three Australian girls who evaded US police inHonolulu while being deported from America wait for another trial for their crimes. A body has been reported this morning lying by the Anahulu River in the Haleiwa Ali'i Beach Park. According to police, two women saw the man lying on the ground in the distance. We're currently patiently waiting for confirmation of whether the man is dead or just unconscious.*

Claudia's hands were shaking as she reached up for the telephone which was near the table. She dialed Joe's phone number and when he picked up, she started talking in great fear.

- Joe, what did you do?

Joe replied with insecurity.

- What? Who am I talking with?
- It's me, you little brat! What did you do?
- I don't know what you're talking about.
- Bastard!

Claudia hung up and started crying.

III.

The Police Station
3 December, 1947

At the police station, Lieutenant Phil More held a press conference about the found body. Questions were coming across the entire room.

- Lieutenant More, Honolulu Paper repoter Mandy Simmons speaking.Do you know whether the found man is just unconscious or dead already?
- Our police officers should be here any minute now. Just be patient. In either case, this situation has to be investigated.

- Lieutenant Phil More, Waikiki News reporter Liz Anderson.What's the investigation going to look like?
- That's a good question, Missus Anderson. It depends on whether the found man is dead or just unconscious. If it turns out that the man is just unconscious, our police officers will interrogate him when he regains consciousness. That's all I can say at the moment.

Lieutenant More heard a car pulling up to the building. With a sigh of relief, he stated.

- Oh, it sounds like our police officers are here.

After a short moment, two police officers entered the room and spoke.

- Lieutenant, could we speak with you for a moment?
- Of course. Just a minute, folks.

Lieutenant More went out of the room along with the police officers. They closed the door on their way out and started talking in the corridor.

- Lieutenant, the man is dead. It appears that a murder occured last night.
- Hmm... That's what I thought, to be honest. I mean seriously, unconscious body? Those reporters nowadays are quite delusional.What a bunch of laughable brats! So, who is the man?
- His name is, or rather was, Gilbert Frederich.

Lieutenant More was surprised as this name sounded familiar to him.

- That Gilbert Frederich? Really? He was quite a popular businessman in Honolulu. How come nobody recognised him?
- That's not such a hard question to answer, Lieutenant. He was found facedown. Also, the entire body was wet. It looks like someone either threw it into the river and it washed ashore or someone pulled the body from the water.

- Oh, I see. Call detective Herbie Fox, then. He's the only reliable person I can think of right now. I'm going to finish the press conference.
- Yes, sir.

Lieutenant More returned to the press conference. He continued speaking.

- All right, I have some new information about the body. It seems like a murder was committed during the night.

The journalists slightly panicked and started asking futher questions.

- Mary Smith, Hawaii Today reporter.Who is the murdered man?
- His name was Gilbert Frederich. Yes, we're talking about the popular businessman.

Everyone in the room was shocked. Lieutenant More tried to calm the journalists down.

- Look! Everything is under control! We're going to do our best to find out who committed this terrible crime and that person will be punished! I would like to ask you to remain calm.

- Jane Foster, Aloha Paper.Do you think our security is too loose?

When the lieutenant heard these words, he became angry.

- For crying out loud! What kind of a question is that supposed to be? You know what? I've had enough! This press conference is over! Thank you for coming!

The journalists were surprised and their shouting accompanied the lieutenant's walking out of the room. Afterwards, the lieutenant entered his office with frustration. He sat down at his desk and covered his face with his palms. After a moment, detective Herbie Fox appeared in the office.

- I heard you wanted to see me, Lieutenant.
- Oh, Fox! I wouldn't ever say that seeing you would brighten up my day!
- How delightful, Lieutenant. I think we should slow down, though. You're making me feel uncomfortable!

Lieutenant More laughed.

- Fox, I would advise you to stop making jokes. We have a serious case on our hands and this one is somehow... everywhere.
- What do you mean, Lieutenant?
- Gee, don't you have a radio, Fox? I woke up this morning and it was the first thing I heard. A body was found by the Anahulu River. Those idiots even thought that the poor man was just unconscious. It's one of the stupidest things I've ever heard on the radio. For crying out loud!

The lieutenant grew angry again and Herbie tried to calm him down.

- Calm down, Lieutenant. You can be glad that you haven't seen The Jack Eigen Show on television. I think that you would have a heart attack by listening to the things that guy says!
- Not funny, Fox! Don't try to be a comedian!
- I'm sorry, Lieutenant.

A few seconds of rather awkward silence occured in the office. Shortly after, the lieutenant started talking in a serious manner.

- Anyway, the man who was found is Gilbert Frederich. Have you heard of him? I bet you have, Fox.
- Oh yeah, that businessman. He tried to look like a good and generous fella but deep inside, I think he might have been even more crooked than the others.
- Perhaps. I don't know much about the guy but I met him once. His business partner got into trouble once and he came here to bail him out of the prison cell.

Lieutenant More grew silent for a moment and Herbie asked.

- So, where is Albert Fringe?
- Oh, about that. I'm so busy and stressed out that I haven't even found the time to assign you a partner. Please, Fox, do me a favor and call him. This is his number.

Lieutenant More opened a drawer and took out a piece of paper with Albert Fringe's telephone number on it. He gave it to Herbie. Herbie left the office and went straight to the nearest telephone booth. He dialed the number and a female voice answered.

- This is the operator.It seems the number you are trying to reach is unavailable at the moment.

Herbie waited for a minute and tried to dial the number again. The female voice repeated the message.

- This is the operator. It seems the number you are trying to reach is unavailable at the moment.

Herbie thought to himself.

- Where is Albie? It looks like he's not home right now.

When Herbie tried to dial the number for the third time with the same results, he gave up. He went back to the lieutenant's office. The lieutenant was having a telephone conversation.

- Yes, it's about that new case. Found body by the river. We need another detective to join Herbie Fox. What about Albert Fringe? Is he available?

A few seconds later, the lieutenant continued.

- I see. So what is his name?

...

- Gerald Horwitz. Is he good?

...

- We'll see about that. Thank you and have a nice day.

Lieutenant More hung up and told Herbie.

- Fox, Fringe is on a vacation. You have a new partner.

Herbie got slightly angry.

- I don't like this, Lieutenant. Just a few months ago, you assigned me a youngster who was completely unknown to me and now you're trying to pull it off again with someone else?
- Fox, don't be such a prima donna! Just because you worked alone for so many years doesn't mean you don't need a partner! I'm sorry about that, Fox. Things change. You know, you're not that young anymore! Gerald Horwitz will be fine.

Suddenly, a tall man came to the office. He had short black hair and a strong figure.

- Did you just say my name? Gerald Horwitz, pleased to meet you... Herbie? Harold? Hercules?

Gerald laughed out loudbut both Herbie and More remained silent. Gerald continued.

- Come on, you two old rascals! Give me a little smile!

Herbie was a little uncomfortable and didn't say a word. Lieutenant More spoke with anger.

- Horwitz! What kind of an introduction is that supposed to be? How old are you, anyway?

Gerald replied.

- I'm fifty-five years young, Lieutenant.

Lieutenant More shook his head in despair without a reply. Herbie stated.

- No offense, Mister Horwitz, but you're acting like a moron!

Gerald laughed out loud and placed his hand on Herbie's shoulder.

- Good joke, Foxy! I think I'm gonna call you foxy lady! What a name! Sounds like a great rock and roll song!

Herbie became angry, too.

- Enough, Horwitz! Lieutenant, are you serious? Is this really the guy I'm supposed to work with? Even I don't find it funny. I want someone else as my partner!

Lieutenant More shouted.

136

- Listen! You both are making me angry! Horwitz, stop acting like a child! Fox, try to understand the pressure I'm under and cooperate already! Now, you two will go to the crime scene and start investigating! You probably don't realise that you're detectives and not stand-up comedians! A man was killed yesterday! Get out of my office and go to Haleiwa Ali'i Beach Park! And Horwitz, don't try to make fun of me or I'll make such a great fun of you that you'll cry! Do you understand?

Gerald replied with a serious manner.

- Yes, sir.
- Good! Get out of my face! Both of you!

Herbie and Gerald left the lieutenant's office and went to the car.

- Mister Horwitz, you're the driver!
- All right.

As they were driving, they had a conversation. Gerald started.

- So Herbie, what do you know about this case?

Herbie sighed and replied with a lower tone of voice.

- Mister Horwitz, I don't want to be rude but I don't know that much and it's because of you! Why did you have to act like a little child in the lieutenant's office?

He's a serious man who hates when someone doesn't treat him with the respect he deserves. The same applies to me, you Horwi lady!

- Come on, Herbie. Why are you all so serious? Have a little laught.
- I have no reason to laugh right now, Mister Horwitz. Maybe I would if you were at least funny.
- Don't be so mean, Herbie! You're hurting my feelings!
- Please, if you don't have anything interesting to say, stay quiet.
- You know I'm not going to do that.
- You're such a dork, Horwitz! Who are you, anyway? I can't even remember hearing your name at all! Tell me something about yourself.
- My name is Gerald and I'm a detective.
- Anything more to add, you baby?
- I don't think so.
- Fine. Just drive then and for the goodness's sake, be quiet!

Herbie was surprised when Gerald remained silent. A few minutes later, they arrived at the Ali'i Beach Park.

IV.

The Crime Scene
Ali'i Beach Park

3 December, 1947

Herbie and Gerald got out of the car. The beach park was surrounded by journalists and police officers. Herbie thought to himself.

- Wow, this is probably one of the most hyped cases I've ever encountered!

Gerald took advantage of the journalists and started showboating in front of them. Herbie ignored him and noticed Officer Blake standing nearby. He went to talk with him.

- Officer Blake! Good seeing you here!
- Hello, Mister Fox! Seems just like yesterday when that daisy case got reported!
- Quite frankly, yes! It was just a few months ago. I think it happened in March if I remember correctly.
- I guess. Anyway, who is your partner now?
- Gerald Horwitz is his name. To be honest with you, he looks like an idiot!
- That's strange. That name doesn't ring any bells for me.

- That's exactly what I thought, too! Who is this guy supposed to be?
- Well, he's probably not so bad. Not everyone can be assigned to such a great detective as you are, Mister Fox!
- Thank you for the kind words, Officer Blake. I'm not sure about that, though. Could you tell me anything more about the case, Officer? This Horwitz guy made the lieutenant so angry he didn't even tell me that much.
- Angry? What did he do?
- You know, I didn't say that he looks like an idiot for no reason, Officer. When he came to the office, he was just laughing and making fun of us both - me and the lieutenant. The poor lieutenant was in despair already and then this guy appeared.
- I understand that. Phil More can be pretty moody sometimes. No wonder he made him angry. Nevertheless, I think you might know that the victim was Gilbert Frederich. He was a famous businessman who owned a company called Sunbeam Finances. I'm not sure whether you heard the news or not. It was just yesterday. A rivalry company called Calico took Sunbeam Finances over and caused a bankrupcy.

Herbie thought for a minute.

- That's very interesting. Thinking about it... isn't it possible that he committed... suicide?

- Good question, Mister Fox. It's not impossible. If that's true, the remaining question would be how. I guess the body needs to be analyzed for further clues.
- Of course, Officer Blake. Talking about analysis, have you seen Mister Marston?
- Yes, of course. He's over there by the blue kiosk.
- Thank you, Officer Blake. I'm afraid I have to leave you now.
- All right, Mister Fox. Take care.
- See you, Officer.

Herbie crossed the police line and bent down to the body. When he saw that Gerald was not by his side, he thought to himself.

- Where is that Horwitz guy? I'm afraid there will be a lot of trouble because of that chump.

Herbie observed the body. First, he looked at Gilbert Frederich's head. He noticed the black eye.

- Hmm, a black eye? He was either in a fight somewhere or someone beat him up pretty bad.

He moved on to the pockets of Gilbert's coat. As he was grabbing them from outside the coat, he grappled with his wallet and finally pulled it out. He found a sum of a hundred dollars in it and a Sunbeam Finances business card. Apart from that, there was a picture of him and Claudia inside.

- Let's see. I remember this woman's face from somewhere. If I'm correct, this woman is his wife.

Herbie put the picture inside his coat pocket and continued searching Gilbert's pockets. Apart from the keys from his home, he couldn't find anything.

A few moments later, Dean Marston came to Herbie and spoke to him.

- Mister Fox!

Herbie stood up and replied.

- Mister Marston! I was just about to come and talk to you! What are your observations so far about the body?
- To be honest, this case appears to be bizarre.

Herbie was surprised and asked curiously.

- Why?

Marston bent down to the body and started explaining.

- You see, the body appears to have several wounds on it. It seems like the victim was punched by somebody. I find it strange that the body washed ashore. What is it doing here? You know, the only reasonable explanation would be someone pulling it out the body out of the water. I would even say that it could be suicide. But still, it doesn't make sense, I guess.

Herbie thought for a minute.

- Mister Marston, I think we have an interesting case in our hands. Have you heard anything about Gilbert Frederich in the news recently?
- Yes, I have. Haven't you?
- No, I haven't.
- You see, the main reason why I think it may be suicide is because of what happened to this man.

Herbie grew curious.

- What happened, then?
- Gilbert Frederich owned a cash loan services company called Sunbeam Finances. I think you're aware of that, am I correct?
- Yes, how couldn't I be? That company was so heavily promoted just a few months ago. Everywhere I went, there were flyers about him and the company.
- Yes, that's correct. Something happened just yesterday to the company. Does the name Calico ring any bells for you?
- I think I've heard about it somewhere.
- It's a rival company to Sunbeam Finances. Well... it was.
- Did they go bankrupt?

- Hmm, no. Calico took over the market. On the other hand, Sunbeam Finances did go bankrupt, indeed!
- How could something like that happen?
- If I remember correctly, Calico took over all the clients that Sunbeam Finances had somehow. Strange, I know. But business can be sometimes harsh and strange.
- That's true, Mister Marston. Have you heard anything about his wife Claudia?
- Let me think, Mister Fox. I remember her appearing on the radio a few times.

Marston tried to remember something he had heard about Claudia Frederich but he could only come up with one thing.

- Mister Fox, I can't remember much, just this: I think she mentioned on one show that she and Gilbert can't have children.
- That sounds interesting. Maybe it had something to do with his death, don't you think?
- Nothing's impossible, Mister Fox.

A few moments later, Gerald appeared.

- Herbie, why are you so modest, rascal? I've just had an interview with about five of the journalists here. You can be grateful, Herbie. If I wasn't here, they would surround you instead of me.
- Really, Horwitz? What did you tell them when you know even less about the case than I do right now?

- I have my ways, Herbie. Come on, trust me. Have a little faith in me, rascal! Who is this nice guy?
- This is mister Dean Marston. He performs autopsies at the police station.

Gerald and Marston shook hands.

- Nice to meet you, Mister Marston. My name is Gerald Horwitz. Your job is awesome! Observing dead bodies... you must be a tough fella!

Marston smiled and replied.

- Thank you, Mister Horwitz. I'm pleased to meet you, too!

Herbie joined the conversation.

- Well, at least you dealt with those journalists, Horwitz. Also, it's nice to know that you have some respect for Mister Marston. Anyway, Mister Marston, who do you think would be the best to visit first for the investigation?
- I would say Gilbert's wife. She was probably the most important person to Gilbert, I suppose.
- Horwitz, do me a favor. You heard Mister Marston. Go and find out the address of a woman called Claudia Frederich, will you?

Gerald stated.

- Herbie, you look so charming when you give commands, rascal! All right, I'll go and get it for you.
- Good, Horwitz. Stop with the jokes already!
- Yeah, yeah, Herbie.

Gerald went to talk with the officers to find out Claudia's address. Meanwhile, Marston and Herbie continued talking.

- That guy gives me headaches already, Mister Marston.
- Oh, come on, Mister Fox. He's just immature, that's all. I suppose you can be glad that someone doesn't take himself so seriously. I think it's a nice change.
- I was hoping for that young fella, Albert Fringe. I found him to be a good partner. A bit quiet, but that's how I like it, to be honest.
- And where is he, Mister Fox?
- Apparently, he's on a vacation right now.
- I see. Where did he go?
- I don't know, Mister Marston. I just hope that this Horwitz guy won't cause any trouble. His first impression wasn't very good, you know.
- Don't you worry, Mister Fox. I'm sure it'll be fine.
- I hope you are right, Mister Marston.

A few seconds later, Gerald came back with the address.

- Here it is, Herbie. The address of Claudia Frederich.

- All right, thank you, Horwitz. You're driving. See you around, Mister Marston.
- Come to my office tomorrow, Mister Fox. I'll have the analysis for you.
- Sure thing, Mister Marston. Goodbye.
- Goodbye.

Gerald said goodbye to Marston, too.

- Bye, you awesome toughie!

Marston laughed quietly and replied.

- See you around, Mister Horwitz.

Herbie and Gerald got into the car, leaving the crime scene.

V.

Claudia Frederich
3 December, 1947

A few minutes later, Herbie and Gerald arrived at the house of Gilbert Frederich. They got out of the car and knocked on the door. Eventually, Claudia opened it.

- Detective Herbie Fox. Claudia Frederich?

Claudia replied with fright.

- Yes. Yes, that's me. What do you want?
- We're investigating the murder of your husband, Gilbert.
- I see. This is probably not the right time but come on in.

Herbie and Gerald entered the house.

- I'm just going to get you a cup of coffee, detectives. Sit down on the sofa in the living room.

When they entered the living room, there was a man sitting on the sofa. It was Joe Pentham, Gilbert's business partner. He spoke to the detectives.

- Greetings, detectives.

Herbie was surprised and asked.

- Who are you?

Joe replied.

- My name is Joe Pentham. Together with Gilbert Frederich, I ran a company called Sunbeam Finances.
- Detective Herbie Fox. This is my partner, Gerald Horwitz.
- Pleased to meet you, detective Fox.

Claudia came inwith two cups of coffee in her hands.

- I hope you don't mind. My friend Joe has just came to visit me.

Herbie replied.

- It's all right, missis Frederich. Besides, we don't have to visit Joe separately now, I suppose.

Claudia put one cup of coffe on the table. She placed it in front of Herbie. She kept the second one in her hands and started drinking softly. Suddenly, Gerald shouted.

- Where is my cup of coffee? I thought the other one was for me!

Herbie looked at Gerald with anger.Claudia was surprised and replied.

- Ex... Excuse me? Why are you shouting at me?

Gerald shouted even loudlier.

- I want coffee! Now!

Claudia got annoyed and stated with antipathy.

- Just a minute, detective.

Claudia went to the kitchen. Joe started speaking.

- That was quite rude, detective!

Gerald replied with a shout.

- Shut up!

Herbie told Gerald with great anger.

- What the hell are you doing, Horwitz? Are you out of your mind?

Gerald remained silent. Joe stood up and went to the kitchen. Herbie continued talking.

- Horwitz, change your behavior immediately! You're nothing but trouble!

Suddenly, Herbie heard an argument coming from the kitchen. He became curious.

- Can you hear that, Horwitz? Sounds like those two are arguing about something in the kitchen!

Herbie tried hard to distinguish the words, but he wasn't able to. After a while, they both returned from the kitchen. Claudia gave Gerald a cup of coffee. Herbie asked a question.

-    Have you just been arguing back there?

They both smiled and replied to Herbie.

-    What? Oh, no, no...

Joe continued.

-    We were just... discussing something. No argument or anything like that.

Herbie was suspicious and stated.

-    All right then. Sit down. Both of you. I would like to start.

Claudia and Joe sat down. Herbie continued after he pulled out his pen and a notebook. Gerald started drinking.

-    Usually, I would leave the writing to you, Mister Horwitz. However, I don't think it's a good idea. Anyway, missis Frederich, tell me exactly what happened yesterday.

Claudia sighed and started talking.

- It's... really difficult for me to talk about it right now. Joe went to work early in the morning and returned much sooner than usual. When he got home, he was very nervous and told me what happened to the company. I didn't know what to say. He said he was going to take a walk and he didn't come home all night.

Claudia was upset and her mood was getting worse. Herbie asked further.

- Can you think of any possible places where Gilbert could have gone?
- Let me think. He liked hanging out in the Lopez Hills Bar. Sometimes, he went out bowling with some of his colleagues. I'm sorry, I really don't know.
- I see. Well, nevermind. How was your marriage with Gilbert? Were you a happy couple?
- Of course we were. Gilbert was a really nice and generous man. I loved him so much...

Claudia started wiping tears off her face. Suddenly, Gerald spoke.

- Whoa! Sorry lady but this coffee tastes like murder! Get it? Murder? But seriously, horrible!

Herbie replied in anger.

- Horwitz! I swear, one more stupid sentence from you and I'll file a complaint!

Joe supported Herbie by adding his two cents.

- Why are you acting like such a jerk? I'm no one to judge you but you really look like an idiot! And Claudia... just stop that!

Claudia looked at Joe with surprise and responded with tears in her eyes.

- What are you trying to say, Joe?

Joe started shouting.

- Come on, don't pretend that you're such an innocent woman! You only married Gilbert for his money!

Claudia cried even more and stated.

- Why are you shouting, Joe? You're hurting me!

Joe continued.

- Yes, just keep your little theater going, Claudia! I'm sick of you!

Herbie shouted, too.

- Enough already! You! Joe! Can't you see that this poor woman is in tears? I'm no one to judge the

154

situation yet but that's not very nice of you! Come on, it's your turn then! Tell me about the company!

Joe calmed down a little and started.

- I met Gilbert in college. We became best friends and we wanted to start our own business. Basically, any business. One day, my family fell into debt. Our bills were overdue and my mother did something very dangerous to keep our home. She borrowed money from a loan shark. A few months passed and we still weren't able to pay our debt. I remember it like it happened yesterday. I was only nineteen at the time. I came home and my mother was nowhere to be seen. She was killed.

Joe became very upset as he continued.

- That day, I swore to my mother's grave. I gave her my honest vow that I wouldn't let this happen to other poor families. Gilbert and I started to work at the local restaurant as waiters. We wanted to earn as much money as possible to start a cash loan business. Luckily, we were successful. That's how Sunbeam Finances was formed.

Herbie claimed.

- That's a very sad story, Mister Joe. Tell me, what happened to the company just a few days ago?

Joe replied.

- A few months ago, a new company started to provide cash loan services. This company is called Calico. Martin Kipp is the founder. He comes from a very rich family. His promises were big. A new modern cash loan service with zero risk for the clients. I don't know how Kipp is able to do what he does. His offers are really extraordinary. If we wanted to try the same methods in our company, we would go bankrupt in just a few days. Anyway, you probably know where I'm heading. Our company simply couldn't match the standards of Calico. It all ended when Kipp offered our clients a switch to Calico for no extra fees, whatsoever. He was successful. We didn't even know what was going on and suddenly, we had no clients! I was thinking about a lawsuit with Calico but it would be a very bad idea. We have no chance against his lawyers. He's too powerful.

Herbie asked further.

- Although it does indeed make sense, I think it's a bit strange. Did Gilbert lose all of his money?

Claudia replied.

- Yes, detective.

Herbie wondered.

156

- But how?

Joe tried to answer Herbie's question.

- It's... quite difficult to explain, detective. Our financal system was, more or less, a house of cards. When Kipp took over our clients, their loans remained our debts.

Herbie tried to figure it out but he was still not sure.

- I'm sorry, Mister Joe. I still feel like there's something missing. I've heard about Gilbert Frederich before. He was quite famous and it has been said that he was wealthy.

Joe claimed.

- That may be true, detective.

Herbie got suspicious.

- Excuse me, Joe. Are you trying to tell me that you don't know whether that statement was true? You said that you were best friends just a few minutes ago!

Joe was a little nervous already and became uncomfortable.

- Yes... I mean, no. Listen, Gilbert was indeed a rich man. The situation with Calico got out of control and it's very complicated to explain why Gilbert lost his money.

Joe stood up and grabbed his coat.

- Excuse me, detectives. I would rather go now, if you don't mind.

Herbie got confused and replied.

- Well, I think that's everything I need to know for now. Although I have to say, Mister Joe, this may not be the end of our conversation!

Joe replied with a fright.

- All right, detective. See you around. Bye, Claudia.

Joe left the house. Herbie continued the interrogation with Claudia. Even though she still had tears on her face, she had stopped crying.

- So, Missus Frederich. I'm glad to see you're not crying anymore. I would like to excuse my partner for making a scene earlier. He feels sorry about it. Right, Horwitz?

Herbie looked at Gerald with anger. Gerald replied with insecurity.

- Yes, Herbie. I'm sorry, Claudia.

Claudia responded.

- Don't worry about it, detective. At least you were honest about my coffee.

Gerald remained silent and Herbie continued.

- All right, let's move on, missis Frederich. I'm curious. Why was Joe visiting you right now?

Claudia replied.

- We wanted to talk about what happened to Sunbeam Finances. It's unfortunate but I need help. We have some unpaid bills and I'm unemployed.

Herbie thought about it for a few seconds and responded.

- I see. But one thing... how could Joe not lose his money from the bankruptcy?

Claudia claimed.

- That's an easy question, detective. It may sound unbelievable but being a manager at Sunbeam Finances wasn't his only employment.

Herbie got surprised.

- Really? What's his second employment?

Claudia responded.

- He's also an executive manager at Ride-O-Mobil company. They sell used vehicles.

Herbie was even more surprised.

- Is that so? Did Gilbert know about it? Besides, why didn't Joe lend some money to Gilbert? He had enough to do that, I suppose.
- I don't know whether Gilbert knew about it. Joe likes to have some secrets. About the money, I think that Joe would lend him some. He knows the best what it means to experience poverty. I really can't tell. Either way, me and Gilbert never talked about Ride-O-Mobil together.
- I understand. There's one thing that concerns me, missis Frederich. My friend heard a radio show in which you appeared as a guest. He told me that you stated how you can't have children with Gilbert. What can you tell me about that?

Claudia was surprised.

- I honestly don't know what you're talking about, detective.

Herbie grew suspicious and replied.

- Are you sure, missis Frederich? Don't lie to me!

Claudia became terrified and responded.

- I'm being honest, detective! Please believe me!

Herbie stated.

- All right, missis Frederich. I believe you. I think we're finished for now. Did Gilbert have any relatives living nearby?

Claudia thought for a minute.

- Yes. You can either visit Gilbert's brother or his sister.

Herbie replied.

- Good. Could you please give me their addresses?

Herbie gave his pen and notebook to Claudia. She claimed.

- Of course, here they are.

She wrote the addresses in the notebook and returned it to Herbie. He stood up from the sofa and went to the door with Gerald.

- Thank you, missis Frederich. Take care. Horwitz, let's go.

They left the house and got into the car. Herbie told Gerald.

- You know what, Horwitz? I've had enough for today. Take me home, please. I'll give you directions.

- Ok, Herbie. What terrible coffee back there, huh? I would arrest her just for that taste.
- Horwitz, please... I have a headache already.

Claudia was looking out of the window. When they were gone, she picked up the phone and dialed.

- Hey! It's me!

...

Me! Claudia, you moron!

...

You don't say! Listen, they have already been here.

...

Yes, exactly! You should take care of yourself.

...

Why are you asking me? I'm not the one to tell.

...

Suddenly, someone rang the doorbell.

- Oh, I have to go now. Someone's here.

She hung up the telephone and went to open the door.

VI.

Herbie's Apartment
3 December, 1947

A few minutes passed and Herbie was home. With several envelopes in his hands, he opened the door and put them on the table. Then, he took a shower and cooked himself an omelette. Before he sat down and started eating, he turned on the radio.

- *Honolulu, it's Waikiki News reporter Liz Anderson! Today, the whole city is shocked by the sudden death of a local businessman, Gilbert Frederich. With Detective Gerald Horwitz by my side, I'm going to ask him some questions!*

Herbie thought to himself.

- Oh, for goodness' sake!

- *So Gerald, tell me about yourself.*
- *Well, Liz, I'm just a warrior against crime! That murderer doesn't stand a chance when I'm on the scene!*

The reporter laughed.

- *Wow, Gerald! You sound really confident about yourself!*
- *Come on, Liz. I'm just doing my job! Stop flirting with me!*

The reporter laughed again.

Herbie got annoyed and turned off the radio.

- Gee! Finally!

When he finished his omelette, he started opening the envelopes. In one of the envelopes, there was a letter. Herbie began reading.

- *Dear Father,*

  It's me, Philip, your son! I haven't heard from you for so long! I wanted to say how sorry I am for everything I've done. I know I wasn't a good son. It's been too long. You probably won't believe me but I miss you. I miss you very much. My life in France is good these days. This place is different from America but I like it. It's been hard during the war, though. I had to jointhe army, too. Luckily, I survived and kept my family safe. Judith and I got married! We have two children! One of them is a little girl called Julia and the other one is Inés! You know, Inés is a common name in France. Julia is six and Inés is two! That's right! You've been a grandfather for a few years already! I'm so sorry, Dad. I thought of writing to you much earlier but I just couldn't find the courage after all I've done to you. Maybe you've wanted to do the same but you didn't have my address. Dad, I wanted to ask you something. We have enough money to come to Hawaii now. It'll be Christmas soon and I would like to spend it with you! Please,Father, forgive me. I'll understand ifyou don't think it's a good idea. Just please, write me a letter.

Sincerely yours,

Philip.

P.S. How's your work?

Herbie was shocked. His thoughts scattered in his mind.

- This is unbelievable! Philip! He's alive! I'm a grandfather and I didn't even know about it! I have to write him!

He stood up from the chair and grabbed his pen and a piece of paper. After a little while, he took a deep breath and started writing.

Dear Philip,

I simply have no words regarding your letter. I'm still shocked by the things I've just read from you. After so many years, you have decided to get in touch with your father. First, I want to tell you something, son. I love you! No matter what happened between us, you will always be my son. Second, I understand your lack of courage to get in touch with me before, but son... You should have written me a letter the day I became a grandfather! It was very impolite of you to keep something like this a secret for so long! What would your poor mother think if she found out about this? Anyway, I'm really glad that you wrote me. Seriously, I thought you were dead, son! About your offer for a Christmas visit, you're welcome to come here! I haven't heard from your brother and sister for a while now. Nevertheless, it's still a very nice thought spending Christmas with my family once again!

Love,

Herbie (your dad, in case you forgot my name).

P.S. My work is fine. I'm currently investigating the murder of a famous local businessman, Gilbert Frederich. You have probably heard about it in the news.

Herbie read the letter once more with his hands shaking.Finally, he put it in the envelope. He wrote Philip's address by looking at the envelope in which he had sent his letter. A few minutes later, Herbie went to the post office and sent the letter. Even though he felt slightly miserable after so much news from Philip, he also felt happy for what had happened.

A few hours passed and Herbie was at home relaxing. After another few hours, he went to bed.

VII.

The Police Station
4 December, 1947

It was ten o'clock in the morning when Herbie arrived at the police station. As he was walking down the corridor, he met Gerald.

- Horwitz! Fine, you're here already! Let's go to the lieutenant's office.

Gerald replied.

- Ok, Herbie.

They both went to the office. Lieutenant More was sitting in his chair waiting for them.

- Fox! Horwitz! How's the investigation going? Any progress?

Herbie replied.

- Yes, Lieutenant. We interrogated Gilbert Frederich's wife, Claudia and his business partner, Joe Pentham.
- Good, Fox. Are you two getting along well?

This time, Gerald replied.

- Yes, Lieutenant. We're like brothers already. If Herbie was Mozart, I would be... uh... Mozart's songwriting partner?

Herbie and the lieutenant looked annoyingly at Gerald. A few seconds later, Herbie added his two cents.

- As you can see, Lieutenant, Gerald is still acting like a child.

Lieutenant responded with an angry look on his face.

- I see that. Fox, could you please leave us alone for a minute? Don't worry, it won't be long.

Herbie went out of the office. He sat down on a chair in the corridor and waited. Meanwhile, he heard the lieutenant's shouting. He thought to himself.

- Hmm... sounds like he's in trouble.

After a few moments, Gerald fiercely opened the door and shouted.

- Great! My work here is done!

Herbie was surprised and went to the office. Lieutenant More was very angry. With a burst of anger, he told Herbie in sorrow.

170

- Fox! I'm sorry but... I'm really not feeling well. This is just too much for me! I've decided that Horwitz is no longer your partner.

Herbie surprise grew. He felt angry but also confused.

- What do you mean, Lieutenant?

While the lieutenant was grabbing a bottle of scotch, he replied.

- You heard me, Fox. Forget about Horwitz! You're on your own from now on!

Herbie didn't know what to say. In confusion, he tried to persuade the lieutenant.

- Lieutenant, I don't know if this is a smart decision. It's true that I prefer to work alone on things but this case is just too serious. Horwitz may not be that well-mannered but he helped me out a little yesterday. If he wasn't with me at the crime scene, I would have been surrounded by journalists!

Lieutenant stated in a bigger anger than before.

- Don't be so stressed out, Fox! That guy is an idiot! Believe me, it'll be better without him! Just try it out, will you?

Herbie replied with insecurity.

- I'm still not sure about this, Lieutenant.
- Come on, Fox! You'll be fine! Just go!

Herbie sighed and responded.

- All right, Lieutenant. I guess you know what you're doing. Take care.

Herbie left the office and went out of the building. When he got in the car, he thought to himself.

- Gee, am I really supposed to drive now? Let's see, where should I go?

He looked at his notebook.

- Hmm... Claudia Frederich stated that Gilbert liked to hang out in the Lopez Hills Bar. I'll trythere, I suppose.

Herbie started the car and drove to the Lopez Hills Bar. When he got inside, there was a middle-aged barkeeper behind the counter. He was an obese man with short black hair. Herbiewas uncomfortable because he recognised him. They had had a rough argument on Herbie's last visit.When the barkeeper saw Herbie, he shouted.

- Hey! It's you again! You're that lousy detective from a few months ago! What do you want?

Herbie approached the bar and spoke to the barkeeper.

- I have a few questions for you, my beloved barkeeper.

The barkeeper was surprised and replied with a smile on his face.

- Are you investigating some murder again? I swear, you're probably the only man in this town who never comes to drink here. At your age, that is. Come on, let me serve you a glass of fine scotch! I'll answer your questions. This one is on me!

Herbie wanted to refuse the barkeeper's offer but when he saw the bottle of scotch, he couldn't seem to resist. He was surprised by the kind offer, too.

- Well, I have to calm down a little, anyway. All right then, you can do that!

The barkeeper served Herbie a drink and gave him the glass.

- Here you are, fella. So what do you want this time?

Herbie sipped the drink and replied.

- Have you heard about the murder of Gilbert Frederich?

The barkeeper thought for a minute and responded.

- Yes. Oh, I see where this is going. You're correct, he was here two days ago.

Herbie was surprised and sipped for the second time.

- Really? Come on, tell me. What was he doing here?

The barkeeper laughed.

- What are you doing here right now, detective? He came here to get drunk, just like everyone else!

Herbie laughed quietly and stated with a smile. He sipped the drink for the third time.

- You're right! You know what? Give me another glass! I like this!

The barkeeper served another drink of scotch to Herbie. When he gave it to, he told him.

-    Here you are, detective. This one is on you, though.

Herbie started to look angry and claimed.

-    All right, all right, my barkeeper, just give it to me!

Herbie finished the first glass and started drinking from the next one. Afterwards, he finally started asking further questions about Gilbert's visit.

-    What did Gilbert Frederich tell you when he was here?

The barkeeper replied.

-    That guy was miserable. He complained about a lot of things. About his company's bankruptcy, about his wife, he whined a lot about his friend. He also complained about some lousy breakfast his wife served him that morning. He said it made him throw up several times that day. Afterwards, he got drunk and before I knew it, he was gone.

Herbie grew curious.

-    What did he say about his wife?

The barkeeper thought for a minute and answered the question.

- Let me see. Yes... he complained about their marriage. He said they were arguing a lot and he was thinking about a divorce.

Herbie was surprised and stated.

- You have to be kidding me! What else did he say?

The barkeeper continued.

- He complained about how they couldn't have any kids.

Herbie was shocked. He finished the second glass and shouted. His signs of intoxication were apparent.

- Unbelievable! Now, give me another drink!

The barkeeper wondered about Herbie.

- Really, detective? Another one? You're beginning to look like an Irishman, fella!

Herbie became irritated.

-   Oh, come on, my beloved barkeeper! I want to drink! These glasses look empty!

The barkeeper served Herbie another drink. Meanwhile, Gerald came into the bar. When he saw Herbie, he shouted.

-   Whoa! Herbie man! Good to see you here, man! Bartender, give me a nice glass of dry Martini!

The barkeeper was curious.

-   You two know each other?

Gerald replied.

-   You bet! We are warriors against crime! Ain't that right, Herbie?

Herbie laid his head on the counter,feelingexhausted. He just mumbled.

-   Mmm...

Gerald told the barkeeper.

-   You see! He confirmed it!

The barkeeper shook his head softly and stated.

-      Two detectives drinking on the job... That's quite sad.

Gerald became angry and replied.

-      Whoa, whoa, whoa, bartender! You have a problem with that? Say that to my face!

Herbie woke up for a moment. When he saw Gerald shouting at the barkeeper, he tried to fall asleep again. Gerald continued.

-      Pal, say a word about me or Herbie, here, and we'll kick your ass!

The barkeeper started shouting, too.

-      You want to go outside? Okay! Let's fight, you two chumps!

Gerald shouted at Herbie. He tried to wake him up.

-      Herbie! Wake up! We're going to rumble! Herbie! Come on, rascal!

The barkeeper laughed and stated.

-      He ain't gonna help you, pal! Don't be a wuss! Let's go!

Gerald and the barkeeper went outside and started fighting. A few moments later, Herbie woke up and began to feel much better. When he saw the fight, he was surprised.

- What... what happened here? Horwitz? Oh no...

Suddenly, one of the people in the bar approached Herbie.

- Mister Fox? May I speak with you for a moment?

Herbie replied.

- Of course. What would you like to tell me?

The man continued. He was a young, skinny-looking man with round glasses and short brown hair.

- I've heard that you're investigating the murder of Gilbert Frederich. I was here two days ago. I can give you some information.

Herbie smiled and responded.

- That's good news! You can start.

The man started explaining.

- My name is John Hawkeye. I was here before Gilbert Frederich's arrival. When he entered the bar, he looked devastated. He ordered a glass of vodka and soon after, he was ordering more and more glasses. He complained a lot about his spouse,Claudia.

Herbie interrupted John's testimony.

- Yes, the barkeeper told me that already just a few minutes ago. What did he say about his friend Joe?

John continued.

- He felt angry with him. He wondered how his business went bankrupt without him doing anything about it.

Herbie thought for a minute.

- Interesting. Did something happen when he was here?

John replied.

- Actually, yes. He got into a fight with the barkeeper, just like your friend here now.

Herbie was surprised.

- You have to be kidding me! How did that happen?

John explained.

- The thing was, Gilbert was drinking a lot two days ago. When he had to pay, he wanted to put it on his tab. The barkeeper refused to do that. Gilbert tried to explain that he lost all his money but the barkeeper didn't believe him. A moment later, the barkeeper asked Gilbert to go outside with him. It looks like he beat him up pretty bad. The strange thing was, it took about twenty minutes before the barkeeper returned. Gilbert wasn't with him anymore.

After a short moment, Gerald and the barkeeper returned. Herbie stood up from his chair and declared.

- Barkeeper! You're under arrest!

Gerald laughed out loud and the barkeeper looked shocked.

- Are you serious, you fat lump? What for?

Herbie replied.

- I've just received information about what really happened here two days ago. You have some explaining to do at the police station! Horwitz! Here are the cuffs. Get him in the car! You're driving to the station. I don't feel so well.

Gerald took the cuffs and used them on the barkeeper. Then, he put him in the police car. Herbie came along soon after and sat in the passenger's seat. During the commute to the police station, the barkeeper grew nervous and started talking.

- Do you know what you're doing, you two suckers? This is not a smart move!

Gerald responded. Herbie wasn't feeling good and he had a strong headache. He tried to remain silent the entire time.

- Don't think you're going to get away with this, bartender! Herbie here is one of the greatest in this town! He knows exactly why you're going to the police station!

The barkeeper tried to threaten Herbie.

- You! Herbie guy! When this is over, you'll regret this!

Herbie felt tired again. He tried to calm down the barkeeper with a softer voice than usual.

- Don't try to threaten me, barkeeper! The testimony was clear! You beat up Gilbert Frederich! We'll just have a little talk at the police station. No one has accused you yet. If you are not the murderer, you can relax.

The barkeeper was still nervous. A few minutes later, they reached the police station. Gerald was leading the barkeeper inside and Herbie was walking besides them. In the corridor, the lieutenant saw them and spoke to Herbie.

- Fox! What is Horwitz doing here? I gave you a clear statement that you're on your own now!

Herbie responded.

- Lieutenant, he's just helping me out with a suspect. I met him by coincidence in Lopez Hills Bar. I probably wouldn't be able to carry him here by myself. I'm experiencing a strong headache right now.

Lieutenant nodded softly and asked further questions.

- All right, Fox. Who is the suspect?

Herbie replied.

- The barkeeper. One of the customers gave a testimony about him. He beat up Gilbert Frederich the night he was murdered!

Lieutenant stated.

- I see. I'll go with you to interrogate him now. Let's put him in interrogation room three.

-

Herbie shouted at Gerald.

- Horwitz! Put him in interrogation room three! We can start the questioning!

After a while, Herbie and the lieutenant went to the interrogation room. Gerald sat the barkeeper at the table and Herbie sat down. Herbie opened his notebook and grabbed his pen. He started talking.

- All right. We can start the interrogation. Did you have any relationship with Gilbert Frederich? Were you two friends?

The barkeeper replied in fury.

- Don't think I'll come off easy, detective! I want my lawyer before saying anything to you! You're not the only one who can play rough!

Lieutenant More started shouting.

- Speak or we'll put you in jail! Don't think you can play with us!

The barkeeper calmed down slightly and responded.

- Ok, ok, chump!

Lieutenant More replied immediately.

- Lieutenant More to you! You're going to treat me with respect, you lowlife!

The barkeeper responded.

- Gee! Ok, Lieutenant. I was Frederich's client. The bar costs me a lot to maintain. That's why I had to apply for a cash loan. I'm not proud of it. Unfortunately, I had no other option.

Herbie was surprised and stated.

- That's good, actually! Tell me about Calico. It's been said that Sunbeam Finances had no clients left when they went bankrupt. Could you give us some insight into this situation?

The barkeeper replied.

- Yes... I can. Just a few days ago, I started receiving letters from Calico. In those letters, they were trying to persuade me to switch from Sunbeam Finances to them. They promised me a ⬜revolutionary plan".

Herbie was curious.

- What was this „revolutionary plan" supposed to be?

The barkeeper answered the question.

- Much lower fees, no extra charges for switching from Sunbeam Finances, no hassle with the corporates, they even wanted to pay one payment for me. It seemed like a fairy tale to me.

Herbie asked further.

- Did you accept their offer?

The barkeeper hesitated about what to say for a moment.

- Well, unfortunately for me... no.

Herbie was curious about the barkeeper's answer.

- What happened to you? Why was it unfortunate?

The barkeeper replied.

- When Gilbert was in the bar... he told me about some unfortunate things.

Herbie became slightly angry.

186

- What unfortunate things? Come on, just say it!

The barkeeper continued.

- He told me that I have a debt. All the money he loaned me became his debt. I didn't understand clearly what he was trying to explain to me. All I knew was... that I'm screwed and I have a huge debt. I might even have to shut down my bar!

Herbie was surprised and something came up in his mind.

- So... that's why you beat him up? What was your reaction to this statement?

The barkeeper replied.

- I was shocked... I became miserable. How was I supposed to react? I wanted to cry... Are you happy now, detectives? The reason why I fought him was... he had about twenty expensive drinks. He couldn't pay for them and he wanted to put it on his tab. I got so mad that I couldn't stand the pressure anymore. He put my whole family into debt. Then he made me another one by not paying. I admit... I told him to come outside with me and I beat him up like a bag of potatoes.

Herbie responded.

- I see. The witness told me that it took you about twenty minutes to come back to the bar. Also, Gilbert was nowhere to be seen. How come?

The barkeeper grew frightened and tried to explain.

- I... We... We were just talking things out for quite a long time. When I punched him, that bastard tried to persuade me how sorry he was for what he had caused me. He cried like a baby. I tried to calm him down. I couldn't just leave him like that.

Herbie was suspicious.

- Something's just not quite right, barkeeper. I'm sorry but... I think you'll spend some time in a prison cell tonight. We need more information before we can let you go.

The barkeeper grew very angry and shouted.

- That's ridiculous! I'm innocent, you bastards! You can't throw me in jail! I have a family and they need me!

Herbie tried to calm the barkeeper down.

- Listen, calm down! You won't spend a long time here if you're really innocent. We just need to verify your testimony with the testimonies of others!

Then Herbie shouted.

- Officer Blake! Come here!

Officer Blake entered the room and spoke to Herbie.

- What can I do for you, detective?

Herbie pointed at the barkeeper and replied.

- You know what to do, officer.

Herbie left the room. Gerald followed him.

- Hey, Herbie! You looked so tough in there!

Herbie kept walking and remained silent. Gerald continued.

- Hey! Herbie! What are you going to do now? Let's get some other punk into jail! Ain't that right? Come on, Herbie! Talk to me!

Herbie replied to Gerald with frustration.

- Look, Horwitz! Thank you for all your help but we're finished. You're not my partner anymore!

Gerald responded.

- But Herbie! We're a great team! You don't need the lieutenant's approval! You know that well! What would you have done without me in that bar? Admit it, we get along well in this job!

Herbie got a little upset and stated.

- Horwitz, maybe you're right... Look, rules are rules. You're not in the game anymore. I'm sorry... This is purely my case now.

Gerald tried to pursuade Herbie a bit more.

- Herbie! Come on! Just think about it, please! I need this job! My family needs it! Talk to the lieutenant. I beg you!

Herbie thought for a little while and replied.

- Well... Horwitz. All right. I'll see what I can do about it. I've tried it already, to be honest with you.

Gerald stated.

190

- Thank you, Herbie. You don't know how much it means to me!

Herbie responded.

- I haven't promised you anything, Horwitz. Just leave everything up to me.

Herbie left the building and accessed the nearest telephone booth. He spoke into the receiver.

- Operator, I need an address! Detective Herbie Fox.

After a little while, a female voice answered.

- This is the operator! Who is the person, detective?

Herbie replied.

- Martin Kipp. Owner of the Calico company.
- Just a minute, detective.

After about a minute, Herbie received the address and got into his car.

VIII.

Martin Kipp
4 December, 1947

A few minutes later, Herbie arrived at Martin Kipp's house. It was a massive villa with a large garden and a fountain placed in front of the door. Herbie couldn't believe his eyes and thought to himself.

- My goodness! I haven't seen such a big house in a very long time.

When arrived at the door, he rang the doorbell. It played a little tune. After a short moment, a female maid opened the door. She spoke to Herbie.

- Si? I mean yes, sir?

Herbie responded.

- Detective Herbie Fox. Is Martin Kipp home, Miss?

The maid replied.

- Si... I mean yes. Come inside.

She led Herbie to the living room and stated.

- Sit down, detective. I go and talk to Sir Kipp.

Herbie replied with a smile.

- All right, Miss. Thank you kindly.

Herbie sat down on the sofa. The maid went upstairs and Herbie heard her knocking on a door, The door opened and he heard her speaking.

- Mister Kipp, some detective is here. He want talk to you.

Martin responded in a terrified tone of voice.

- What? Come here for a minute!

The maid went inside the room and Martin closed the door. Afterwards, Herbie heard a glass breaking and indistinguishable shouting. A little while later, Martin came down the stairs. He was a middle-aged man with short brown hair and a thin figure. He wore a blue sweater and black trousers. As he was coming down the stairs, he spoke to Herbie.

- Mister Fox! Glad to meet you!

Herbie stood up as Martin approached him and they shook hands. Martin continued talking.

- It's a pleasure to meet you, Mister Fox. I know why you're here, to be honest. I've been expecting you.

Herbie replied.

- Good to know, Mister Kipp. Without further ado, let's start.

Herbie opened his notebook and grabbed his pen. The maid brought a cup of tea.

- Have some tea! Very good, lemon tea!

Suddenly, Martin shouted.

- Thalia, for goodness' sake! Can't you see we're having a serious conversation here?

Herbie was surprised and stated.

- It's all right, Mister Kipp. I would love to have a cup of tea, Miss Thalia!

Thalia looked happy when she heard Herbie's words. Herbie took a cup of tea and sipped it. Then, he continued the conversation with Martin.

-   Mister Kipp. Let's begin then. Tell me about your relationship with Gilbert Frederich. Did you two know each other?

Martin smiled and replied.

-   Of course. I can't say we were friends, though. We met a few times on various occasions and that was pretty much it.

Herbie asked further.

-   What about his business partner, Joe Pentham?

Martin answered the question.

-   Joe... now that's a whole different story! We're good friends! Honestly, that man is on his sure way to the top!

Herbie was curious.

-   What do you mean by that?

Martin responded.

-   He's a powerful and solid businessman. I see a lot of potential in that guy! I even loaned him some money so he could start his car company, Ride-O-Mobil!

196

Herbie was surprised.

- Is that so?

Martin replied.

- Yes. I've seen the reports. No regrets!

Herbie continued asking questions.

- That's odd. I have some more serious questions for you now. Tell me about your company, Calico. How did it start out?

Martin grew a little frightened and started explaining.

- It's a business I started just a few months ago. We provide cash loan services. It all started when a good friend of mine complained about Sunbeam Finances.

Herbie thought for a minute.

- Really? Who was that friend of yours?

Martin got nervous and tried to change the topic of the conversation.

- That's not important, detective. Let's move on, shall we?

Herbie grew suspicious immediately.

- Why can't you tell me, Mister Kipp? Was it Joe? Don't lie to me, Mister Kipp!

Martin got very frightened and responded.

- Yes... I mean no! Ok, it was him.

Herbie started raising his voice slightly.

- What did he complain about, Mister Kipp?

Martin remained silent for a short moment. Herbie stated.

- Tell me, Mister Kipp. You don't have to hide anything from me. Either you tell the truth or I'll find out another way, and in that case, it'll be worse for you!

Martin broke down.

- All right, all right, detective! I'll tell you everything! Joe complained about Gilbert. All the time! He thought it wasn't fair that Gilbert was the boss and not him! He said that Gilbert wasn't responsible enough to lead such a powerful company. You know, Joe always wanted to be the boss. Gilbert didn't let him havethat position. Never! I'm about to tell you something very confidental now.

Herbie was curious.

- What is it, Mister Kipp?

Martin took a deep breath.

- One day, Joe called me. He wanted me to...

Martin seemed to be too afraid to finish the sentence. Herbie pushed him into it.

- Come on, Mister Kipp. You can do it! Finish the sentence, please.

Martin took another deep breath.

- He wanted me to hire a gunman for him. He asked me to... kill Gilbert.

Herbie was shocked and shouted.

- You... you just can't be serious! What a scumbag!

Herbie stood up, intending to call the police to arrest Joe. Martin stopped him.

- Please don't do that, Mister Fox! It was a long time ago! Joe got over the fact that he couldn't be the boss of Sunbeam Finances soon after that incident!

Herbie hesitated but agreed. He realised that the interrogation was not over yet. He stated.

- All right, Mister Kipp. Let's finish this interrogation before making any assumptions.

Herbie sat down again and the conversation continued.

- Mister Kipp, there is one thing that really concerns me about Calico. How is it possible that it took over all of Sunbeam Finances clients?

Martin smiled and replied.

- I guess you can ask that question of our clients, Mister Fox. I don't know why they decided to switch to our company. Our only strategy was to build a fair marketing plan to inform the citizens of Honolulu about us. Nothing that special about it.

Herbie thought for a minute about the statement. He continued asking questions.

- What about the clients who didn't switch to your company? I have testimony from one person about the situation. He stated that he didn't switch from Sunbeam Finances to your company and that caused him a huge debt. Can you say something about that, Mister Kipp?

Martin thought about it. After a short moment, he stated.

- No, I can't, Mister Fox. This is quite surprising for me to hear. I thought that all of their clients switched to Calico. In any case, it sounds reasonable. If someone didn't make the switch before the bankruptcy occured, he suddenly carrys the company's troubles on his shoulders. How could a bankrupt company loan someone money? Think about it. Can you give me some contact information for the unfortunate person? We can help him pay off the debt.

Herbie responded.

- That's very kind of you, Mister Kipp. I'll let you know when that person turns out to be innocent. It doesn't look good for him at this moment. Let's move on now. What can you tell me about Gilbert's wife Claudia? Do you know her?

Martin replied.

- Just as much as I knew Gilbert. Maybe even less, actually. Gilbert introduced us at one of the events we both attended. She's a beautiful lady, I have to say. We had a little conversation and that was all. Surprisingly, she told me about her problems with Gilbert. She was thinking of divorcing him at that time.

Herbie was surprised and stated.

- That woman told everyone the truth except me! Why would that be?

Herbie started thinking. Martin responded.

- It's not surprising, Mister Fox. Have you heard any of the radio shows she appeared on? When asked in public, she always lied about her marriage with Gilbert. If anyone asked her a question concerning Gilbert, he was the best man alive and she was the happiest woman on Earth to be his wife. Actually, I can prove it to you! I have a vinyl record of one of her radio interviews! Hawaii Flash Radio had a special sale one day. They were selling various recordings of their shows. Just a moment, I'll set up the phono cartridge and bring the record.

Martin set up his phono cartridge and turned it on. Afterwards, he opened one of his wardrobes and pulled out the recording. He placed it on the cartridge and played it.

- Greetings to our fellow listeners. You're listening to Hawaii Talk. My name is Sam Turkins and I'll be your host for today's episode. Our special guest today is the spouse of famous local businessman Gilbert Frederich, owner of a trending company called Sunbeam Finances. Please welcome Claudia Frederich!

Claudia spoke.

- Good evening to you, Sam. I'm pleased to be on theshow.

Sam started the conversation.

- Claudia, you're such a handsome young woman. How does it feel to be married to such a powerful man of our town?
- It's a lot of joy, Sam. Gilbert is the most wonderful man I've ever met. I love him very much.
- That's very nice to hear, Claudia. It sounds like you're a happy couple. Is that right, Claudia?
- Oh, yes it is, Sam. We're currently thinking about having children.
- That's interesting, Claudia. Anyway, tell us something about yourself. What are your hobbies, for instance?
- I like playing tennis and I have a lot of passion for art.

- *Yes, it is known that you're not too shabby a painter, Claudia. One of your paintings hasjust been presented in the National Gallery, is that correct?*
- *Yes, Sam. I'm very proud that one of my works reached the National Gallery. It's a great honor for me.*
- *What did Gilbert say about your paintings?*
- *Honestly, he doesn't like them very much. I'm just kidding, he loves them! He was very happy when I told him about the presentation of my paintings at the gallery.*
- *Wonderful, Claudia. How long have you been playing tennis?*
- *I've played tennis for many years now. Gilbert even bought me my own tennis court. He's such a caring man.*

Martin stopped the vinyl recording.

- I think I have proved my point, haven't I?

Herbie replied.

- Yes, you have. That's quite interesting, I have to say. Needless to say, I'm probably not wondering that much about it. Gilbert Frederich was really quite a popular man here.

Herbie stood up from the sofa and continued.

204

-   All right, Mister Kipp. I think we're done. You're a fine
    man, Mister Kipp.

Martin smiled and responded.

-   I have the same thoughts about you, Mister Fox.
    Thank you for your visit.

Herbie stated.

-   Take care, Mister Kipp.

Herbie left Martin's house. When he was gone, Martin picked
up his telephone and dialed Joe's number. After a short while,
Joe answered and Martin told him in a stressed tone of voice.

-   Joe! Joe! I've just had a visit.

Joe asked in confusion.

-   A visit? From whom?

Martin replied.

-   It was a detective Herbie Fox. Listen, I don't know
    how to say this. I have no idea why but he thinks
    you're the murderer. He was talking about you the
    whole time!

Joe was frightened.

- Me? That's ridiculous. Have you talked with Claudia about it yet? She will lose her mind! I can't go to jail just because some detective thinks I'm a murderer!

Martin answered.

- No, should I? Hang on! Has she found out anything about the will yet?

Joe grew excited and replied.

- Surprisingly, yes! It may be better than we thought it was at first!

Martin replied.

- That sounds good. You should try to run now, though. That detective will be at your house soon!

Joe responded.

- Ok, Martin. Thanks for calling me. Bye.

Martin hung up the telephone.

IX.

Joe Pentham
4 December, 1947

Herbie was driving a police car. He called dispatch to arrest Joe.

- Dispatch! This is Herbie Fox! I need police backup to arrest a suspect named Joe Pentham. The address is 449 Lanipuao Street.

A female voice spoke from the transmitter.

- All right, detective. Sending police backup to 449 Lanipuao Street.

A few minutes later, Herbie arrived at Joe's house. The police backup was there already. When Joe opened the door and saw the policemen, he tried to rush to his car and escape them. His attempt was not successful. Joe was arrested and brought to the police station. Herbie started the interrogation in interrogation room two. Lieutenant More was in the room, too.

- Joe Pentham! I think you remember me. I have some serious questions for you this time! I have testimony which says you attempted to hire a gunman to kill

Gilbert Frederich in the past. What can you tell us about that, Joe?

Joe was frightened. He replied.

- I have no idea what you're talking about! I've never wanted to hire a gunman to kill Gilbert! He was my good friend!

Herbie shouted.

- Don't lie to me, Joe! I know that you've always wanted to be the leader of Sunbeam Finances! Gilbert never gave you a chance and you were frustrated!

Joe was very nervous and tried to persuade Herbie further.

- Yes, that's true, detective! I've always thought that Gilbert was not responsible enough to lead such a huge company. I would never want to kill him, though! I started my own company just a few months ago! I didn't feel the need to be the boss of Sunbeam Finances anymore!

Herbie thought for a minute. Afterwards, he asked further.

- All right, Joe. Let's say I believe you. Tell me now. What is your relationship with Claudia Frederich?

Joe answered the question in great fear.

- We are just friends! I swear!

Herbie was very suspicious. He shouted once again.

- I think you're a pretty big liar, Joe! No! It doesn't seem like the correct answer to me! Officer Blake, go out and bring Claudia Frederich here!

Officer Blake responded.

- Yes, Mister Fox. Just give me a few minutes.

Officer Blake went out of the building and drove to Claudia's house. Meanwhile, Herbie was trying to push Joe even more.

- Joe! I have a feeling that you have kept many secrets from me! Giving a false testimony is a federal crime! Do you realise that? If Claudia Frederich says something different than you, you'll be punished! It doesn't matter if you're innocent or not! Joe, I advise you to tell me truth before Claudia arrives! Come on!

Joe panicked and broke down. He started explaining.

- All right, detective! Do you want the truth? I'll tell you the truth! Claudia and I are lovers! She's wanted to divorce Gilbert for years! Their marriage wasn't happy at all!

Herbie was surprised and asked further.

- I should have thought so! How long have you been lovers?

Joe replied.

- It may be two years. And yes, it is true that I wanted to hire a gunman on Gilbert once! That man was miserable! If he had died back then, I would have been the boss of Sunbeam Finances! It's all gone now! That company is ruined to the core! Claudia thought the same about Gilbert. In fact, she hated Gilbert! She may seem like an innocent and tender woman but she's a devil in disguise!

Herbie wanted to ask more but Dean Marston interrupted the negotation. He entered the room and spoke to Herbie.

- Mister Fox! Good, you're here! You have to come with me! I have a shocking discovery for you!

Herbie responded.

- Yes, Mister Marston. I'm coming!

Herbie left the interrogation room. He went to the laboratory room with Dean where Dean revealed the body of Gilbert Frederich. He started explaining.

- Mister Fox! This was probably one of the hardest bodies for me to make observations about! You see, it was unbelievable for me! There were almost no wounds, no blood on the ground, no signs of sharp objects or anything like that! The only wounds are located on the victim's head and the reason for them is clear already. They were caused by the barkeeper you brought in today! I had to inspect the body further. Look, I found this in the victim's body!

Dean grabbed a small plastic bag with a couple of drops of a dense substance in it. Herbie was curious.

- What is it, Mister Marston?

Dean replied with confidence.

- It's honey! I know what you're thinking. You see, it's not ordinary honey! Not even by a mile! It contains particles originating from rhododendrens, azaleas and oleanders! Mister Fox... this is a deadly poison for the human body! That's our answer! The victim was poisoned! This honey takes about six hours to work. The victim probably consumed it in the morning!

That's why there are no serious wounds, no signs of blunt objects or a drop of blood!

Herbie was surprised. After a minute, he claimed.

-   So the murderer was... Claudia! She... she betrayed her husband! It makes sense! Thank you very much, Mister Marston. I need to go and prove it now. I still don't have enough evidence against her!

Dean stated.

-   How unfortunate! Go, Mister Fox! Make her pay for her sins!

Herbie left the laboratory. In the corridor, there was Claudia being brought to the interrogation room. Herbie returned to the room to finish the interrogation. Claudia and Joe were sitting at the table. Lieutenant More was gone.

-   Well, well, well. Nice to see you, Claudia! I'll get straight to the point. I know about everything, Claudia!

Claudia was surprised and asked with insecurity.

-   About what, detective?

Herbie responded.

- It's over, Claudia! Why did you murder your husband?

Claudia looked shocked.

- I don't know what you're talking about, detective!

Herbie punched the table and shouted very loudly.

- I know about the honey, Claudia! Stop playing games with me! Your lying is over! Why did you do that, Claudia? Why?

Claudia started crying and stated.

- All right, I admit it! I'll tell you! I have something to say about me and Joe!

Joe interrupted Claudia.

- He knows already, Claudia!

Claudia cried even more and continued talking.

- We had a plan together!

Herbie pushed Claudia.

- What plan, Claudia?

Claudia replied.

- The reason why I killed Gilbert was... I found a hidden will of Gilbert's. It promised I would inherit millions of dollars.

Herbie thought for a minute. Something was very unclear to him.

- Wait a minute. Sunbeam Finances was bankrupt! It was stated that Gilbert lost all his money!

Joe tried to explain this time.

- Detective, that was a part of our plan. The truth is... Sunbeam Finances didn't go bankrupt. I found a loophole which meant I was able to shut down the company. I mean... all of the clients taken over by another company? Come on! That doesn't sound real! In fact, Sunbeam Finances was still standing! I saw no point to keep it alive, though. My company Ride-O-Mobil is climbing the ladder every day. Also, Gilbert would never let me be a boss!

Herbie shouted.

- And that's why you had to kill your friend? Because you two were greedy? Shame on you! Tell me about the honey!

Claudia started explaining.

- Joe knew a person who could make poisonous honey. He fed some of his bees on rhododendren plants. All parts of these plants are poisonous. I put it in the cup of tea I gave Gilbert at breakfast. When I heard the news the next morning, a part of me died with Gilbert. I regretted it immediately. I'm sorry to say that you're out of luck, detective... all the honey is gone now. You have no evidence against me!

Herbie responded in anger.

- Don't worry, Claudia! I'll find a way to prove it! I don't know how but I will!

After a short moment of silence, Herbie stated.

- I'm going to the lieutenant's office.

Herbie went to the lieutenant's office. He spoke to the lieutenant.

- Lieutenant! We have the murderer!

Lieutenant was surprised.

-   Fox! That's great news! You can start explaining!

Herbie started explaining.

-   It's Claudia Frederich, the wife of Gilbert Frederich! She and Joe Pentham had a plan! They wanted to kill Gilbert Frederich because of some hidden will. This will promised Claudia would inherit millions of dollars!

Lieutenant thought about it and wondered.

-   But Fox! What about the bankruptcy of Sunbeam Finances?

Herbie replied.

-   That's the thing! There was no such bankruptcy of Sunbeam Finances! It was all just a big lie! Joe managed to shut down the company. He told one that the company went bankrupt! He and Claudia probably wanted to make Gilbert Frederich's death look like a suicide!

Lieutenant asked further.

-   That sounds interesting, Fox. How did they kill him?

216

Herbie continued.

- The answer is honey. Not a casual honey, though! Joe gave Claudia a special poisonous honey made from bees who were fed on rhododendren plants! It all makes sense! The poison takes six hours to start working! The barkeeper told me that Gilbert complained to him about vomiting several times that day!

Lieutenant smiled and stated.

- Great job, Fox! One last question... where is the evidence?

Herbie got a little upset and replied.

- That's the problem, lieutenant. I... have no evidence. Only those testimonies make this conclusion.

Lieutenant got angry and responded.

- For crying out loud, Fox! How are we supposed to win the court case without any physical evidence? You better find somequick! Do you understand, Fox?

Herbie replied in a lowered tone of voice.

-   Yes, Lieutenant.

Suddenly, someone knocked on the door. The door opened and it was Gerald. He was carrying a bag with him. The lieutenant spoke to him.

-   Horwitz! What are you doing here! You have no business here! Get out!

Gerald tried to calm down the lieutenant. He was very calm.

-   Lieutenant, Herbie, I have something for you.

Gerald opened his bag and Herbie lost his mind when he saw the object. It was a half empty jar with a tag ⬜Honey of Death⬜stuck to it. Gerald explained.

-   I found this in Claudia Frederich's house.

Herbie was very excited and asked Gerald.

-   Horwitz! My goodness! How... how did you get it?

Gerald replied.

-   You know, Herbie, you all think I'm an idiot. I'm not! When we went to visit Claudia Frederich together, I knew there was something going on with that woman. Think about it! She didn't even look upset about the death of her husband! Anyway, after our interrogation with the barkeeper, I did something. I went to visit Claudia Frederich once more. This time, I asked her to make me a cup of tea and I took a look around when she was in the kitchen. Soon, I found this jar in one of the drawers. I simply took it and left. One of my friends is a scientist. I brought him a sample and he confirmed my assumptions. This honey is a deadly poison!

Herbie wanted to cry with joy and he shouted.

- Horwitz! I don't know what to say! Thanks to you, we can sentence Claudia Frederich! You're a hero!

Gerald laughed and responded.

- Oh, Herbie! I'm just a warrior against crime, like you! Ain't that right, Herbie?

Herbie smiled and replied.

- Of course you are, Horwitz! Of course you are!

He turned to the lieutenant.

- Lieutenant, you have to give this man his job back! You see how much he did for the case in the end!

Gerald remained silent. Lieutenant More thought about it for a moment. After a short while, he stated with insecurity.

- Well, concerning the fact that... Maybe, just maybe... All right. You got me, Fox! Horwitz, here is your badge! Think twice before doing anything stupid, though!

Gerald's eyes filled with happiness. He told the lieutenant.

- Thank you! Thank you so much, Lieutenant! You won't regret this, I swear!

They all three laughed. After a while, Herbie stated seriously.

- Wait just a moment, fellas. I still need to finish something.

Herbie grabbed the jar of honey and went to the interrogation room. He spoke to Claudia and Joe.

- Claudia Frederich, Joe Pentham, you're under arrest for the murder of Gilbert Frederich!

Herbie showed the jar of honey to Claudia and she became terrified. Herbie continued.

- Officer Blake, arrest them!

Officer Blake smiled and replied.

- All right, Mister Fox.

Officer Blake arrested Joe and Claudia. The barkeeper was set free. When Herbie saw him, he spoke to him.

- Barkeeper! My beloved barkeeper! I'm sorry that you had to spend some time in jail.

The barkeeper smiled softly and responded.

- You better be sorry, detective! I told you I'm innocent! Don't you trust me, detective? I served you a free drink, remember? Chump!

They both laughed and Herbie stated.

- Don't worry, barkeeper! We'll get you out of debt! A good friend of mine promised to help you!

The barkeeper was surprised.

- Are you... are you serious, detective?

Herbie replied.

- Yes, yes, my beloved barkeeper! Talk to you soon! I have to go now. Take care!

Herbie returned to the lieutenant's office. Gerald was nowhere to be seen. Herbie took a look outside and there was a group of journalists.

- Mister Horwitz, Liz Anderson speaking. Nice to see you again! So who's the murderer?

Gerald replied with confidence.

- Nice to see you, too, Liz! The warrior against crime has just won the battle!

When Gerald noticed Herbie, he grabbed him and continued.

- What I really meant to say is, the warriors against crime have just won the battle!

Herbie grew uncomfortable and stated.

- Stop it, Horwitz! Seriously!

Gerald laughed and responded.

- Oh, come on, Herbie! Do it for Liz, please!

Herbie smiled and walked away saying.

- I'm telling on you, Horwi lady! Don't make me do that!

Gerald remained silent for a moment. After a little while, he continued.

- Anyway, where were we? Oh yeah, warrior against crime!

Herbie placed his palm on his face.

A few days later, the court sentenced Claudia to fifteen years in prison. Joe was sentenced to ten years in prison for his cooperation. Martin Kipp bought Joe's company, Ride-O-Mobil. Soon after, it became one of the most successful car companies in Honolulu.

X.

Lopez Hills Bar
23 December, 1947

It was eight o'clock in the evening. Herbie was drinking scotch in the Lopez Hills Bar. The barkeeper spoke to him.

- I want to thank you for helping me out with my debt. That Martin Kipp guy is really something! He even paid some of my debt from his own money! What a good man, that chump!

Herbie was feeling very tired and he stated.

- This scotch is good, barkeeper! I can't stop drinking! What have you done? What have you done, barkeeper?

The barkeeper laughed and replied.

- I made your life less miserable, detective! Seriously, if you put me in jail once more, I'll triple the price just for you!

Herbie fell asleep for a few minutes. Afterwards, Herbie came home. At about 11 o'clock in the evening, the doorbell rang. Herbie went to open the door. It was Philip.

- Dad?

Herbie couldn't believe his eyes. He wasvery happy and shouted.

- Philip! You came! You seriously came!

Herbie hugged Philip strongly and tears streamed down his face. Herbie asked him.

- Where's your family, son?

Philip replied.

- They're in a hotel. I wanted to come and see you for at least a little while. Oh, Richard and Veronica are here, too!

Herbie got shocked even more.

- Richard and Veronica? Does this mean that I'm going to spend this year's Christmas with my entire family?

Philip responded.

- I guess so, Dad.

Herbie cried for a little moment. Philip asked him.

-    Are you all right, Dad?

Herbie assured him.

-    Yes, of course I am. I'm just so happy, Son!

The next day, Herbie had a big Christmas dinner with Philip and his family, along with Richard and Veronica, his other children. It was the first time in years thatHerbie was truly happy.

CHARACTERS CHARACTERISTICS

Name: Herbie Fox

Age: 60

Date of Birth: 27/2/1887

Place of Birth: Honolulu, Hawaii

Job: Detective

Family status: Widowed

Children: Philip Fox, Richard Fox, Veronica Fox-Winsley

Appearance: 5 ft 4.96 in, 209 pounds, gray hair, scar on a cheek

Name: Gerald Horwitz

Age: 55

Date of Birth: 20/11/1892

Place of Birth: Honolulu, Hawaii

Job: Detective

Family status: Married

Children: Andrew Horwitz, Margareta Horwitz

Appearance: 6 ft 1.09 in, 180 pounds, black hair

Name: Robert Wintski

Age: 52

Date of Birth: 20/4/1894

Place of Birth: Kapolei, Hawaii

Job: Bartender

Family status: Married

Children: Sylvia Wintski, Thomas Wintski

Appearance: 5 ft 4.17 in, 247 pounds, short black hair

Name: Phil More

Age: 63

Date of Birth: 25/3/1883

Place of Birth: Honolulu, Hawaii

Job: Lieutenant

Family status: Married

Children: George More

Appearance: 5 ft 4 in, 134 pounds, gray hair

Name: Gilbert Frederich

Age: 43

Date of Birth: 9/11/1904

Place of Birth: Honolulu, Hawaii

Job: Businessman

Family status: Married

Children: none

Appearance: 5 ft 6 in, 170 pounds, brown hair, green eyes

Name: Claudia Frederich

Age: 36

Date of Birth: 29/5/1911

Place of Birth: Honolulu, Hawaii

Job: unemployed

Family status: Married

Children: none

Appearance: 5 ft 8 in, 110 pounds, black hair, blue eyes

Name: Joe Pentham

Age: 42

Date of Birth: 30/7/1905

Place of Birth: Honolulu, Hawaii

Job: Businessman

Family status: Single

Children: none

Appearance: 5 ft 7 in, 157 pounds, black hair

Name: Martin Kipp

Age: 35

Date of Birth: 12/9/1912

Place of Birth: Honolulu, Hawaii

Job: Businessman

Family status: Single

Children: none

Appearance: 5 ft 9 in, 145 pounds, short brown hair

About The Author

Steven Vagovics is a young author from Slovakia. Besides writing, Vagovics showed high interest in music. In 2013, he released an EP album on his own which contained five songs recorded at his home. The album was available for a free download on his website. His LP album is about to be released sometime in 2015. In 2010, he created a YouTube account where he regularly posts his stereo mixes and remasters of the songs by The Beatles. Written in 2014, 'The Mystery of Bloody River' is Steven's second book in the established 'Herbie Fox Stories' series. Steven Vagovics received several awards throughout his elementary school years in English competitions.

www.ingramcontent.com/pod-product-compliance
Lightning Source LLC
Chambersburg PA
CBHW030512020726
47494CB00004B/1068